I0553369

The Guardian

#1 Mended Souls

Jacquie Biggar

"Look, Trace…"

"Don't you 'look, Trace', me." She sighed, and moved to his side. Her fingers sent tingles upward from where they rested on his arm. "You may be used to playing the hero for damsels in distress, but that's not me, okay?" Her eyes were emerald green, mesmerizing in their brilliance. "I'm used to taking care of myself. I don't need coddling."

No, maybe she didn't. But that didn't mean she couldn't use someone to take the burden away. He wanted to be that someone.

He raised a hand and brushed a velvety soft cheek, reveling in her body's response. Eyelids fluttered and lips parted as though waiting for a kiss. Maybe she didn't want the fairy tale, but that didn't mean he couldn't be her prince.

He leaned down and accepted her invitation.

Heaven.

Her taste reminded him of blue skies and endless meadows. Of songbirds and bubbling brooks. She was his fire when he got cold and food when he was hungry. She made him weak, yet superhero strong, all with a look or a touch. And he couldn't get enough.

"Take me home with you," he whispered.

Tracy gazed at him, her eyes conflicted. "We should…"

"What? Slow down? Deny what's happening between us?" He tunneled his hand into her hair and cupped the side of her head, relieved when she leaned into the touch. "I can't. If there's anything I've learned in the past couple of weeks, it's that there are no guarantees."

He leaned forward until their foreheads touched. Until every breath was shared. Until there was no room for misunderstandings.

"I want you."

I have so many people I'd like to thank. First, and foremost my husband, Robert John. Without you I wouldn't have had the courage to pursue my dreams. Thank you, honey.

My mom, who has always been my guiding light and allows me to toss ideas with her. Thank you, I couldn't do this without you.

To my daughter, Brandy, my inspiration to never give up.

To my critique buddies- you know who you are. Without you pushing me to better myself, this book might never have happened.

To my beta readers for their tremendous input, and the reviewers who are key to a writer's success. Thank you.

And last but not least, to Kim Killion and Jennifer Jakes, for the beautiful cover I'm so proud of, thank you.

This book marks my first foray into the paranormal genre. I had a lot of fun world-building and hope you enjoy Lucas, Scott, and Tracy's story.

Jacquie

ISBN: 978-1-988126-04-3

Everyone is someone's devil.

Matthew Hicks

Foreword

From Tidal Falls:

This was truly an enjoyable book to read with just the right amount of suspense, sexual tension, humor, and romance. The drama of the story sucked me in from the first page and the plot twists kept me reading until the thrilling ending that didn't disappoint. Who wouldn't love a book with a strong heroine (Sara), a sexy hero (Nick), an adorable, spunky little girl (Sara's daughter Jessica), a gorgeous group of Navy SEAL team members, a devoted K-9, a sexy and smart DEA agent (Maggie), and a cold, manipulative villain (Tom) who wants to ruin everyone's happiness?

I especially loved the threads of love, friendship, family, and comfort food woven throughout the book. A great start to an exciting series that I can't wait to read!

Jacquie Biggar has a wonderful gift for writing hot and extremely likable military men! I couldn't decide who was my favorite: Nick, Frank, Jared or Adam. Luckily this novel is the start of a series so the good news is that I'll be seeing a lot of these men again in future books by Ms. Biggar. Hooyah!

The Guardian

#1- Mended Souls by Jacquie Biggar

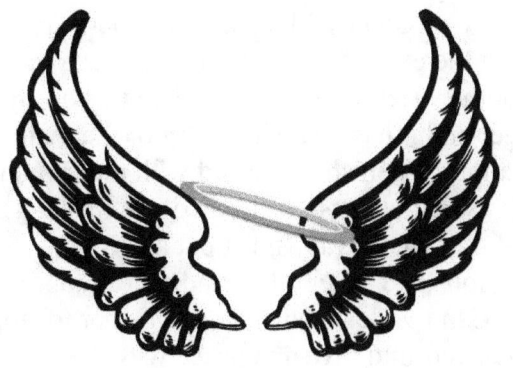

Preface

The premise of this story is that of a couple of free living movie stars who have their lives changed forever when they are involved in a horrific car accident. One dies, Lucas Carmichael, and is left to seek redemption for his carelessness by vowing to help those he left behind.

Scott Anderson is lost and bitter without his best friend and blames himself for the accident. When the ME charged with investigating the case is harassed, Scott tries to help and finds himself caught up in a dangerous web of lies and deceit.

Cook County Medical Examiner, Tracy York, has seen the extreme violence humans can inflict on one another. Her sister was murdered when she was a teenager and it has made her wary of the male population. When she is tasked with the investigation into a suspicious crash that killed one mega-star, and injured the other, Tracy must put aside her reservations and accept the hand of a stranger.

Can two lost souls come together to stop a madman and find love and peace with the help of a sarcastic angel, or will fate deal them a losing hand?

Chapter 1

If Lucas Carmichael had known he was going to wake up dead, he might have kept sleeping.

There was some sort of a thin sheet covering him from head to toe, but it didn't do anything to stop his body from shaking or his heels from vibrating on the table beneath him. His chest pumped like a set of bellows on steroids. He blinked repeatedly to get his bearings, but still couldn't see a fricking thing.

What the hell was going on?

A white-hot pain hit him between the brows.

Ow.

He rubbed his forehead. Except—his palms were still on the cold metal of the table. He could feel them there. So, whose…?

Adrenaline spiked, shooting adrenaline through his system.

Terrified, he shoved off the choking hold of the sheet and threw himself to the floor, crouching for a moment to get his bearings, every muscle tensed. Reaction set in and perspiration broke over his naked body, rattling his teeth. A high-pitched whistle rang in his ears, and his heart pounded harder than his old base speaker beating out a Black Sabbath tune.

He squinted against the lights, blindingly bright after the darkness of the sheet. A man and a woman stood a few feet away behind another table with a blanket shrouded figure. Weird. They hadn't even glanced up when he performed his gymnastics. Something strange was going on here.

"It's too bad. She had her whole life in front of her," the woman said as she took some sort of vise and lodged it in the poor sucker's chest. "I heard they were headed from a party when it happened."

The other guy in a white jacket shook his head. "These guys never learn. They think just because they're the newest hot item and have more money than God, nothing's ever going to happen to them."

He reached into the cavity and carefully removed what looked like the heart and placed it in a pan resting on the corpse's feet. "At least she'll make a good research candidate."

Holy shit.

He was in a freaking morgue. How the hell did that happen? Last thing he remembered was cruisin' down the highway in his new 911 Porsche with the music blaring so loud he could barely hear himself think. His best friend, Scott, with his younger sister, Natalya, on his lap in the passenger seat, had just glanced over her blond head and smiled the quirky grin that had won him instant box office success.

Lucas remembered thinking they were so freaking lucky—to come from where they had, to where they were now? A miracle.

He'd laughed and turned back to the curves of the road, but his vision went wonky for a second. When it straightened out his eyes had widened in shock. The sharp tang of copper flooded his mouth. The windshield was filled with the terrified faces of the family in a van hurtling straight toward them. Shit, he must have swerved over the center line.

They were going to crash.

Time simultaneously slowed to a crawl, and jumped to warp speed. The man was frantically trying to turn the wheel and avoid the collision, while the woman's horrified face stared accusingly at him out the window before she turned to the back seat in a vain effort to protect her babies. Those images would haunt him for the rest of his days.

A litany of prayers Lucas hadn't uttered since he'd been a young child rattled off his lips while Scott's "What the fuck?" vibrated with fear. He felt more than saw his friend bracing for impact, his arms tightening around Nat as he buried her face in his shoulder.

Then there was a horrendous screech of metal on metal. His chest slammed into the steering wheel with bruising force, knocking the breath from his lungs. The momentum propelled the car to skid sideways and collide with the van again, this time from the rear. The collision sent his body smashing against the driver's door. Natalya's scream reverberated and then was abruptly cut off. His head cracked hard against the window. The last thing he remembered was the suffocating sensation of the deployed airbags.

Lucas rose and backed away from those bloody gloved hands doing God knows what to whoever was on that table. He bumped into another tray filled with instruments of torture and froze at the resultant clang. He covered his privates and met the startled gaze of the doc. Except she looked right through him, her pretty green eyes narrowed with suspicion.

"That's not funny, Hank. I told you I don't like your games."

The man, Hank, threw his hands up in the classic 'hold on there' pose. "Hey, it wasn't me this time, I swear." He moved closer to the tools, as though to defend himself with a scalpel or something, the idiot.

The woman's eyes pierced the shadows, only marginally relaxing when she found the room empty. Well, except for the stiffs and him of course. Lucas had a very bad feeling. The only reason for those two not to be able to see him was if he were invisible. And since he was reasonably sure he hadn't received a bite from a radioactive spider, he must be a… ghost.

No sooner did the thought flutter wraithlike through his mind than Lucas' feet lifted from the tiled floor, pulled up by a brilliant white light encircling his body. He groaned, the heat a benediction on his aching bones. So it was true, there was another realm after death. He'd always believed when he died, that was it. He'd become just another shit-stain on the fabric of mankind. It's how he'd lived his life, no harm, no foul. But, this. This felt… divine.

If there really was a heaven, he didn't deserve a spot. Not after everything he'd done.

It seemed like only seconds later the beam transported him to a textured surface sort of like the topping on his favorite dessert of lemon meringue pie. There were hills and hollows all in creamy shades of tan and white as far as the eye could see. It made him queasy.

He looked around but didn't see another soul, living or otherwise. *N*ice to know he hadn't lost his rather dubious sense of humor when he died.

Christ.

He was dead.

The stark truth hit him and drove him to his knees. Little tufts of cloud bounced crazily, temporarily obscuring his vision. Not that he was missing much; he was the only freaking person up here.

Was this his fate then? To spend an endless eternity wandering around the perimeter between this world and the next, not allowed to enter either dimension? It was no more than he deserved, but he'd give anything to know what happened to Scott, Natalya, and that family. He didn't care what lay in store for him as long as they were okay.

Please.

A sensation crept over his skin like a warm breeze. Someone was watching. His head flipped around like *Beetlejuice*, searching the ever-changing monochromatic landscape around him, but there was nothing.

And then, suddenly—there was.

A figure appeared out of the mist. Completely covered in a glowing white robe from head to toe, the ethereal body floated across the distance and came to a halt about a metre away. The… thing stood with its head bowed and arms crossed in front of him. He could have easily passed for an albino monk.

Holy shit.

If Lucas wasn't dead already, this place would have done the trick. He'd never been a fan of fun houses. The creepy mirrors, moving floors, and freaky characters appearing out of nowhere pretty much negated the whole *fun* aspect.

He rose on unsteady legs and waited with his heart in his throat, ready to turn tail and run if that robe uncovered a creature from his nightmares.

"Who are you? Why am I here?" he demanded.

The guy rocking the bed sheet fashion accessories wasn't talking. Why was this happening? Okay, he got it. He'd fucked up, nut it was a little late to do anything about it. If he was dead, fine. Drop him in a hole somewhere and leave him the hell alone.

This is bullshit.

"We agree."

The words, spoken in a soft baritone, seemed to enter his head without ever being uttered. Lucas raised his hands for protection against he knew not what. His heart threatened to bounce from his chest. He closed his eyes and prayed to a God who'd never listened that he was just in shock and this was all a bad dream. It had to be. But when he chanced opening them a few moments later, nothing had changed. It seemed this was to be his new reality.

"Come," the voice said. Without waiting on his compliance—though really, where was he going to go—the figure turned and drifted over a nearby peak.

Lucas hesitated, torn between throwing himself over the nearest cloud-bank, and trailing behind to see just what the future held in store for him.

Curiosity won. He followed.

Chapter 2

Cook County Medical Examiner, Tracy York, finished writing up the last of her reports and leaned back in her ergonomic office chair. Stretching her aching back, she contemplated the Chicago city skyline. It was her job to determine cause of death and bring closure to families grieving the loss of loved ones, but today had been tough. She was beat.

Some cases were harder to handle than others. Today she'd stood aside and bore witness to a woman's gut-wrenching pain at the loss of her husband and unborn child while the man who caused the injury lay just a few feet away. No one had stepped forward to mourn his death. Tracy couldn't say who she felt sorrier for—okay, yes she could. It angered her that a family had been torn apart all because some idiots who were too stupid to know alcohol doesn't mix with driving had decided to take their party on the road.

Scott Anderson and Lucas Carmichael.

Of course she'd heard of them. Who hadn't? Both were riding a wave of success from their latest action movie. Both were notorious playboys the paparazzi took pleasure in chasing. Now one was dead, and the other… well, he wouldn't be performing his own stunts for quite some time.

She didn't get out to the movies very often, but she had a DVD player and her own stash of late night indulgences starring Scott Anderson. Her lips quirked over her teenage-like crush on the man. She remembered her relief when he and his super-model wife divorced last year. As if he'd ever have an interest in someone like herself, a science nerd.

Lucas had a blood alcohol level of .07 at the time of the crash. It was enough to mess with his depth perception, reasoning, and peripheral vision; all of which probably slowed his reflexes to the point that he couldn't react fast enough to correct his mistake when he crossed the center line of the highway. Eyewitness testimony and evidence on the scene corresponded with Tracy's analysis, not that it made her feel any better. This was one time she could have gone without being right.

The woman they'd performed the autopsy on yesterday was said to be Anderson's sister, out from California for a visit with her movie star brother. Guess she got more than she'd bargained for with these two. She didn't have a chance; at the moment of impact she'd flown through the windshield and died of internal hemorrhaging.

Tracy sighed. The media attention outside the office was crazy and her boss was not a happy camper. There was a lot of pressure coming down the pipeline to make her findings disappear. It wouldn't look good for the movie's promoters if they were backing *a couple of baby-killers*, as the tabloids were calling them.

She knew Gil wouldn't bend under the pressure. He swore by the integrity of his office. But there'd been some threats lately that neither of them could take lightly. From prank phone calls warning them to change the outcome or else; to typewritten notes left on generic paper with no prints, pasted to the windshield of her car while parked in front of her home. The police were looking into the matter, but without hard evidence there wasn't a lot they could do.

She slipped her heels back onto her aching feet and rose to wander around, not anxious to go home to her sterile condo. Life in the city might be exciting, but it was also damn lonely. Besides, she liked being in the office when everything was soft shadows and cool silence.

Drawn to the drawers where they stored the decedent's bodies, she tugged on the second one from the end, the one where Lucas Carmichael lay at rest. She carefully turned back the white sheet from over his face and chest. Other than a nasty gash from where his head hit the side window, he seemed as though he were simply taking a nap. His hair glinted a rich coffee brown with streaks of bronze that picked up the light and complimented his Hollywood tan. There were deep lines at the corners of his eyes that suggested a hard life. A tribal tattoo covered his left pec and a vine of thorns wrapped his arm from elbow to shoulder. No wonder he'd been so successful. Even dead she could feel his charisma.

Where Lucas had come across as sarcastic and intense, Scott was the ever light-hearted counterpart. The contrast played well on the big screen and the two were often paired up in movies. With Scott's wavy blond hair and crystalline eyes, it was easy to see why the women flocked to his side. There was a certain way he had of gazing out from the screen that made every female under sixty believe that look was solely for them. Even though she knew better, Tracy had felt the flutter of her pulse more than once over a tub of Ben and Jerry's Chocolate Chip Cookie Dough and a certain surfer guy movie star. Nothing said a girl couldn't dream.

A cool sensation grazed her jaw and startled her out of her reverie. She glanced around, expecting someone to have entered the lab, but the room was silent. Uneasy, she started to flip the cover over Carmichael's face, but something halted her movement. Hesitating, she shook her head and tucked the sheet around his shoulders instead.

"I've definitely been here too long. Now the corpses are sending me messages." She slid the steel drawer shut, ignoring the inner voice that insisted she leave it open. "I should book some time away, now that this case is done. A vacation sounds heavenly."

She couldn't remember the last time she'd taken time off work. Between getting her degree and shipping any extra money she earned back home to her mom and young brother, there wasn't a lot left for extraneous activities. Not that it mattered. Gil was always giving her a hard time for being a work-junkie as he so eloquently called it. The reality was much more banal; she didn't have anything else to do.

The dating scene just wasn't her thing. The couple of relationships she'd had since moving to the windy city had ended amicably enough, and she remained friends with both men. She just wasn't one for passions of the heart. Much better to logically pick her dates based on common interests and mutual attraction. More than one of her friends had been in so-called love, only to have it crash and burn because they had one without the other. She wasn't going to make that mistake.

Tracy opened the bottom drawer in her desk and removed her one extravagance, a gorgeous Burberry satchel, and dug to the bottom for her keys. Time to go home and soak her aching feet. She opened the door and cast a last pensive glance around the room before shutting off the lights. Her heels clicking on the tile seemed overloud in the hushed silence of the building. Heart rate matching her speed, she hurried to reach the elevator. Her finger stabbed the down button and the doors opened as though waiting to gobble her up.

She hesitated, then stepped into the slightly cool interior, lips quirking at her crazy imagination. Back against the mirrored wall she waited for her stomach to drop with the fall to the underground parking garage.

All too soon the elevator glided to a halt and released her into the clutches of the concrete jungle outside its doors. At least the parking garage was well lit and had a security code access, so she felt relatively safe walking the length of the row to her car.

Tracy sighed, relieved when her little Honda Civic came into view. She hated to admit it but the threats had bothered her more than she let on. She clicked her key-fob, reassured by the flash of the headlamps.

Then she noticed the bloody mound laying in front of the car.

Tracy screamed.

Chapter 3

Scott Anderson wished he were dead.

His head hurt like a bitch. He had two cracked ribs and his right arm was broken, but he'd take double that pain if only it would bring his sister and his friend back.

Natalya and Lucas—gone.

The agony ripped through him like a tornado, destroying everything in its path. They'd been compadres since grade school and took care of each other—always. But he'd dropped the ball, and now they were dead.

He gazed around the private room, large and airy with potted plants meant to break up the sterility, and leather furniture as plush as you'd find in any high-end hotel. Only the steady beep of the monitor beside his bed and the IV stuck in his hand betrayed the fact this was a hospital. That and the two-hour checks on his condition, as though he were a child in need of supervision.

He had to get out of this place.

"I don't need you poking and prodding me every time I close my eyes." He'd glared at the woman, who bore a striking resemblance to *Broom Hilda*. "You've already shown me the panic button at least ten times. I'll call if I'm in distress or need someone to hold my dick while I piss, otherwise leave me the hell alone."

She'd ignored him while she took his pulse, checked his eyes, and plumped his pillows. Then she wrapped the cuff around his good arm and pumped up the pressure until he thought his skin would split open.

"There's no need to be rude, Mr. Anderson." Whoosh, the air released and he sighed his relief. "We're trying to do our job and you're not making it any easier." She took note of the numbers, wrote them on the chart, then unwrapped the stethoscope from around her neck and placed the cup near his heart.

He sucked in a quick breath at the coolness of the metal and raised his eyebrow. She shrugged and smirked. The witch.

"Deep breath, please." She listened for a moment, then moved the instrument to his side and slid carefully beneath the bandages. "Again, please." Finished, she checked his fingers under the cast for swelling, then covered him with the blanket and lowered the glare of the light above the bed. "Try to get some rest. I know this must be a difficult time…"

Scott turned away, blinking hard against the rising tide of anger and despair. She patted his shoulder and moved away to the door. He watched her in the reflection off the windows until she left the room, then threw back the sheets and clambered awkwardly out of bed.

Shit, that hurt.

Immediate guilt flooded his chest. How dare he whine about a little bit of pain when his family lay in steel boxes. And it was all his fault. Lucas didn't even want to go to that stupid after-party. The whole thing had been his idea. Get out; be seen.

He'd spent so many years building up their public relations image; he didn't know when to quit. They'd both been hungry for success, anxious to blow away the stink of where they came from. And now, just when they'd achieved victory, it had all been taken away.

In a fit of rage he yanked the needle out of his hand, barely noticing the tug of the tape on his skin. Anxious to find some clothes and escape, he stepped forward and almost did a face-plant. His legs wobbled like a newborn foal's; he had to fight to remain upright. His ribs screamed at the enforced pressure and his arm in the cast felt like a gazillion pounds.

He swore, pissed at his weakness. For a second he hung his head and just breathed. Lucas wouldn't have let a few bruises slow him down. Scott almost smiled; remembering the many scraps the two of them had back home. They'd been the scrawny trailer trash kids, never mind that the rest of the boys on the block came from the same sort of background. The only good thing that place did for them was put a fire in their bellies, a determination to succeed so they'd never have to go back.

Now it was just him.

Scott straightened, at least as much as he could, and using his casted arm to brace his side, he shuffle-stepped to the closet by the bathroom. Score;

his freshly washed clothes were neatly hung on the hangers. Now the trick would be to put them on without passing out.

Hunger gnawed like a ravenous beast at Lucas' insides. He hadn't had anything to eat since the morning of the party and it was starting to catch up to him. He wasn't exactly sure how long he'd been… you know, but going by the low growl in his belly it had to have been a while.

"Hey," he called to the figure floating—yeah, like that wasn't weird or anything—a few feet ahead of him. "Where does a guy go to get some food around here?"

It all looked the same, a sea of foaming white in every direction. Already, he missed the bright lights and city noise, the fresh Santa Ana breeze blowing against his face, a warm woman's body in his arms.

But most of all, he missed Scott.

His friend would blame himself. Scott had been the mother hen of the three, the peacekeeper. Friends as far back as Lucas could remember, they'd been warriors in kid's shorts, fighting imaginary dragons and real life demons. He didn't care so much about himself, but he needed to make sure Scott would pull through okay. There had to be a way.

Maybe he could become a guardian angel, or something. Him, an angel. As if that wasn't the biggest oxymoron of the century.

And speaking of angels; he better hurry up or he was going to get left behind. He'd yet to see the face of the robed figure in front of him. The guy wasn't exactly a chatty Cathy either. He'd tried a couple of times on their seemingly never-ending pilgrimage to get him to say something, but so far, nada. Hopefully they weren't all like that up here, or he was going to go stir-crazy.

"So, you got a name?" he asked, damn near jogging to keep up. Maybe he should ask for wings instead of food.

"You have to earn them." There it was again; the voice that wasn't a voice.

"Quit doing that, man. You're spooking me out, here." As though everything else he'd been through in the last while wasn't enough to raise the old goosebump-o-meter.

"What are the chances that this is just a supremely shitty dream and I'm going to wake up in the morning with the king of all hangovers?"

Nothing.

"Yeah, I thought not."

Just then they topped about their fifth rise and lo and behold, a small wooden building appeared near what almost looked like a Thomas Kinkade lake scene. The closer they got, the better it smelled. Someone was pan-frying fish over a campfire. Lucas' mouth salivated.

The scent took him straight back to happier times, just after he and Scott had left home and were making their way to Hollywood, land of the rich and famous. They had no real cash so they'd chosen to camp out rather than waste their money on hotel rooms.

One night the two of them camped by a lake the color of the finest of emeralds. The fishing was great, and they'd feasted on trout and grayling with a bread chaser.

Manna from heaven, Scott had said, laughing. He'd been right.

Lucas' stride lengthened, his pulse clamoring to know who was doing the cooking. They rounded the corner of the cabin and there, in front of the dancing flames, sat a wizened old man with a flowing white beard and shoulder length hair. Lucas stumbled to a halt.

"Move, don't make Him wait," the omnipresent voice whispered through his mind.

"It's okay," the old guy said, his gaze on the fish sizzling in the cast iron frying pan. "It is rather a lot to take in. Give the boy a little time."

Lucas felt like a kid. He wanted nothing more than to run forward crying, throw himself on the ground, and beg His forgiveness. The kindness and gentleness emanating from the man reached out and embraced him in a warm hug, giving him the strength to greet his Lord.

He dropped to his knees and bowed his head in shame. He had no right to be here, in His presence.

"You're right, you don't," his cheering squad of one muttered in his ear.

"Enough," the Maker sighed. "You two need to learn to get along. You're going to be working together."

"What?" Lucas and the monk voiced their dismay as one.

The Lord smiled. "Better, you're already thinking alike." He waved to the overturned logs on the other side of the fire. "Have a seat gentlemen, it's time we got down to business."

He waited for them to take their seats. "Lucas, what you did was wrong."

Lucas snorted, *no kidding*.

"Don't get smart." Monk man again.

"Too late, at least I can come up with words that contain more than one syllable."

"Stop now." The Lord glanced up, his eyes a cloudy sky blue. "There's no time for your bickering. People you both care about are in danger. Your assignment is to keep them alive. Help them find peace. Agreed?"

A vision appeared. Scott and that woman doc from the morgue were running through a dark forest. Shots were fired. Scott was limping. The woman tried to help him, her arm around his waist, but then she went down. The look of anguish on his buddy's face drove Lucas to his feet.

The image evaporated and he was left staring into the fire.

Shit.

He looked up and met his new partner's gaze. They took each other's measure, and then the monk nodded.

"Agreed."

The Lord just smiled, as though he'd known the outcome all along.

"Fish anyone?"

Chapter 4

It was dark by the time Scott managed to get dressed and make his way out of the hospital, careful to keep the hat he'd borrowed from another patient pulled low over his eyes. His hand had already risen to wave down a cab before he remembered he'd need cash. He patted down his pockets, relieved when he felt the welcome bulk of his wallet. It must have been returned to him after the accident.

"Where to?" The driver glanced his way and then focused on the clipboard in his hand.

"West Harrison," Scott panted, breathing through the pain of bending to slide into the car.

The gray head turned and concerned eyes met his. "You okay?" The cabbie nodded toward the hospital. "Maybe you better head on back and let them check you out."

One glimpse of the crowd of reporters milling around the entrance and Scott turned away. "I'm fine, just get me outta here."

The man hesitated, then shrugged and started the meter. "Whatever you say, boss."

As they pulled from the curb a guy wearing a dark shirt and pants moved away from the group, a cell phone plastered to his ear. Scott's gaze passed over him, then returned. There was something...

"Car accident?"

He jumped, his gaze snapping to the cabbie's curious scrutiny in the rear view mirror. "Why do you say that?" he demanded. His pulse throbbed at his temple. Then he realized the man was referring to his cast and bruises. He sighed. "Yeah."

He leaned his aching head against the back of the seat and closed his eyes. Immediately visions of a white van hurtling toward them filled his mind. Lucas grimly trying to avoid the collision; Natalya screaming as he pushed her head into his shoulder As though hiding her was going to delay the inevitable. He remembered thinking it was going to be all right. Lucas would fix this, he always did. Then the crash came and the world went black.

When he awoke, their agent, Ray Farrell, was there to inform him he was lucky to be alive. Three others hadn't survived. And Scott somehow knew his sister and best friend were gone.

The car slowed to a halt.

"We're here, A."

Scott's eyelids flipped open, his heart stuttered, and he sat up too fast, grunting at the ache in his side. "What did you just call me?" he demanded.

A weirdly familiar set of eyes again met his in the mirror. Then the cabbie pointed out the front window at the imposing cement structure of the Medical Examiner's office.

"I just said we're here, man. This the place you wanted?" He leaned forward to stop the meter and Scott's gaze landed on the cross gently swaying from a silk tassel below the mirror. A warm sensation flowed into his belly and washed all his anxieties aside. He must have heard the man wrong.

"This is it. What do I owe ya?" Scott lifted his hip and extracted the wallet from his back pocket, careful not to jar the cast or his ribs.

"Twenty will do. Are you sure you got the right place? This is the morgue, ya know."

Scott winced. His mouth straightened into a hard line. "I'm well aware of where we are, yes." He passed the cash over the seat and opened his door. "I'll be about an hour. Can you come back and pick me up? There's an extra fifty in it, if you do."

He climbed out of the car without waiting for a reply and slammed the door. Frustration was eating a hole at his insides. He hated when something was there, skirting the edges of his mind, but not allowing him to figure it out. Lucas had given him a hard time more than once for his lack of patience. He'd always been mercurial though; that's why the two of them had meshed so well. Lucas was the calming brook, while he'd been more like the raging rapids in their relationship. The whole carefree persona he carefully portrayed for the benefit of the public was just that, a guise.

He watched the taxi until its taillights disappeared around the corner, then reluctantly limped toward the double glass doors lit by a yellowish glow from recessed lighting. The breeze ruffled his hair and snuck past the collar of his jacket to send a chill down his spine. He grimaced and yanked the loose side of the coat closer around his body. He'd been lucky that the t-shirt he'd been wearing at the time of the accident was loose enough to slide his arm through with the cast, but there was no way his coat would fit unless he sliced it, and he'd refused to do that. The Blue Jays jacket came from one of the last baseball games the two friends had attended together. They'd shared a love of the sport and had a friendly rivalry going every year on who would make the finals. Lucas was a White Sox fan all the way, so he'd gone out in left field and chosen the Jays as a sure way to rile his buddy. The game they'd attended; Sox won seven-six, and Lucas had crowed about it all the way home. The asshole.

He swallowed the lump in his throat and tugged on the door, but it didn't budge. He rattled it a couple more times before he noticed the hours of operation on the side window; eight-thirty to four-thirty, Monday to Friday. Well, that figured. It was—he checked his watch—ten p.m. and Friday night to boot.

He sighed, relieved and frustrated in equal measure. Now he had two more days to wait before he could say a final farewell to his buddy, at least in private. The funeral was sure to bring a crowd, Lucas was—had been—a star. And Natalya… a shudder shook his frame. His little sister… gone. He couldn't imagine never seeing her sparkling blue eyes as she teased the hell out of him again. He and Lucas had always protected her, kept her safe. They'd never wanted her to go through the same pain they had.

Head suddenly too heavy for his shoulders, he turned away from the darkened building and wandered down the sidewalk. Guess he had some time to kill before the cab came back. At least it was quiet here, away from the downtown core and prying eyes. The tension slowly eased as the meds kicked in and dulled the pain so he could finally breathe without it feeling as though his lungs were getting squashed. He'd had bruised ribs before, but the ache from these two cracked ones made that seem like a holiday. At least he could feel the pain; his buddy was beyond that now.

The sense of loss overwhelmed him and his eyes grew blurry. It was so damn hard to envision a future without Nat and Lucas. They'd come from dysfunctional families; Lucas to an abusive father. Scott and Nat to a set of parents who didn't even know they were alive half the time. They had become each other's family. He punched the tree he'd taken shelter beneath, ignoring the sting of freshly scraped knuckles. It wasn't fair. It wasn't freaking f...

A woman's scream from somewhere around the corner interrupted his pity party. Scott was on the move before the sound died down. He wiped his eyes on his sleeve as he jogged down the walk as fast as he could, cradling his arm to his side for support. His heart pounded out a staccato beat in his chest and he probably looked like the *Hunchback of Notre Dame* with his weird gait, but it couldn't be helped.

Rounding the corner he skidded to a halt and frantically searched the area. Where was she? Away from the bright lights of the entrance, this side of the building was darker, more ominous. He edged down the block, keeping to the shadows, his breathing loud and erratic.

Might as well announce yourself.

He could almost hear Lucas' voice in his ear and grinned. It got wiped off his face a second later when another gut-wrenching scream split the air. It resounded from the parking complex on his right. He raced for the entrance, pulling up short against the gate blocking the passageway. An overweight man in ill-fitting guard clothes was stepping out of the ticket booth. He jumped at Scott's sudden arrival.

"Have you called the cops?"

The guy shook his head. "Don't want no trouble. The boss said to keep things quiet, and that's what I'm doing."

Scott swore. "Let me in. Someone needs to help that woman." And when the guy didn't move fast enough, "Hurry up, or I'll make sure your boss knows what an ass you are."

The guard hesitated, as though debating whether to comply or not, but then he shrugged and hit the remote so the gate would lift. As soon as there was room, Scott ducked through, adrenaline dulling his pain. He ran for the lower floor, praying he was heading in the right direction. At the same time, he pulled his phone out of his pocket and dialed 9-1-1.

"What's your emergency, please?" A woman's impersonal voice carried into the garage and Scott hurried to lower the volume.

"I need help. There's a woman in some kind of trouble. She's screaming, but I haven't found her yet to tell you why."

"Name, please."

Scott stared at the phone. What the hell? This wasn't a social call, for crying out loud. "Look, it doesn't matter who I am," he whispered, slowing now that he was in the bottom row. "Just hurry up before something bad happens. The Cook County Medical Examiner's Office. In the garage. Hurry."

He hung up before she could say anything more and angled his way past a couple of parked cars and a meridian. That's when he found the woman. She was crouched over something on the ground in front of a gray Honda.

Maybe he shuffled his feet, or she just sensed he was there, either way she turned and looked right at him with the biggest, greenest eyes he'd ever seen. They provided a stark contrast to the sight of her blood-soaked hands.

Chapter 5

Tracy stared up at the stranger a few feet away, on the edge of hyperventilating. Was she going to be the next to die? Every instinct shouted for her to get the heck out of there before she became the next victim, but empathy urged her to stay, defend the dog who had done nothing to deserve this punishment.

The man stood in the shade of the cement pillars, a cap pulled low over his forehead blocking his features. She had very little to protect herself with other than a set of keys she'd dropped in her haste to help the injured beast, and a small can of mace she kept in her jacket at all times. It would have to do.

"Are you all right?" The slightly winded cadence of his voice didn't inspire confidence. He raised a hand, as though to calm her, and she let out a squeal.

Too late, she was officially freaked out.

Her heart fluttered against the walls of her chest; a butterfly caught in a jar with no chance of escape. She hysterically wondered if Hank would be the one to do her autopsy.

"Miss, I asked if you needed help?"

He sounded harmless, but then, the Boston strangler's victims probably thought the same thing.

"Who are you? How did you get in here?" Impossible to tell for sure from where he was standing but Tracy didn't recognize him as one of the many employed in the building. She'd worked here for five years and knew almost everyone—at least by sight.

He moved forward a couple of feet, the shadows casting broad stripes across his torso. The artificial lighting caught in curls at the nape of his neck, turning them an antique gold. Though she crouched, he seemed tall, well over six feet. His frame was lean and lanky, a runner maybe with those strong-looking legs.

Good thing with his line of work.

If things weren't so serious she would have smiled. Nothing like a little gallows humor. A sad little whine tugged her gaze to the mangled pup. He was coming around. Elated, she traced shaking, bloody fingers along the animal's muzzle in an effort to reassure him she meant no harm.

"Hush, little one. You're going to be just fine," she murmured, and hoped she wasn't lying. Soft brown eyes with absurdly long lashes stared up at her filled with hurt and bewilderment. "I know, you didn't deserve this, you poor thing." She'd used her scarf to wrap the wound and staunch the flow of blood, but it was only a temporary fix. The dog needed help, and soon.

The stranger appeared on the other side of the pup, startling both of them. Tracy palmed the mace and held it up, warning him away. "Get back. This stuff burns. I don't think you want to feel its effect." The dog growled low in his throat, its body tensed.

He ignored them to crouch with an odd grunt, and run his hand over the mangy coat. The dog snapped, his teeth gleaming a dull yellow.

"Relax, boy. I'm not here to hurt you," he said. "You, or your master." He glanced up from beneath that ugly cap and speared her with ice-blue eyes. "Were you injured?"

Tracy pulled herself out of the laser beam intensity of that gaze and realized he meant her bloodied hands. She shook her head. "No, I found him this way. It couldn't have happened very long ago or he'd be dead. That's why I thought maybe you were…" She shrugged, feeling a little sheepish now that her nerves were settling. He didn't look like the serial dog killer type, but that didn't stop her from keeping the mace at the ready.

He sat back, seemingly offended. "You think I did this?"

Now that he was closer, she noticed his arm was in an Orthopedic cast and that reassured her more than anything else could have. Not very likely a man with a broken arm would be able to attack a dog and deposit him in front of her car without getting any blood on himself.

"I don't any more," she muttered, her nervous gaze doing another loop of the area. That meant the real perpetrator was still on the loose.

The blood on her hands was drying now, leaving them covered in a thin film like when she used to use school glue for decoupage and managed to get it on her fingers. As the paste dried she would dig with her nails until the edge lifted and then peeled way from her skin, quite often coming away with an outline of her prints in the cast. Great fun—unlike now.

"You never said; how did you get in here? This is a gated garage." She kept a wary eye on him while checking the dog's dressing. "We need to get this guy upstairs so I can help him."

"You? Are you a vet, then?" He looked her up and down, the doubt obvious in his expressive face. "I called the emergency number when I thought it was you in danger, they should be here soon. Your gate-keeper, who let me in by the way, can show them where to go."

Her knees were cold from kneeling on the cement. It couldn't be good for the pup. She worried he might already be going into shock. "Give me your jacket, we need to get him warmed up." Tracy tugged her own coat off her shoulders and tried to ignore her companion's appreciative stare. If there was one thing that made her self-conscious it was her over-developed breasts. Men took one look and figured her for a cheerleader—or a stripper. Neither one was acceptable. And it wasn't that she was a snob, because she wasn't. Women in those trades were usually more out-going, socially adept. Tracy wasn't. After what happened to her sister… well, she just wasn't.

The dog seemed to realize the humans were trying to help him. He gave up struggling and lay quietly when she laid her coat and the stranger's jacket over his soiled fur. She rubbed his black and white head and glanced curiously at the man watching them.

"Do I know you? You seem familiar?" His angular face reminded her of someone, she just couldn't put her finger...

"Holy smokes," she squeaked. "I know who you are." She was surprised it had taken her so long. "You're Scott Anderson, aren't you?" Okay, this was officially the craziest day on record. Heat raced up her neck and made her ears hot with embarrassment. He must think her a raving idiot. Accusing Scott Anderson of animal abuse—nice.

He shook his head, then sighed and removed the cap. "I guess the jig is up." Then, the weirdest thing happened; his whole demeanor changed from kind and sincere, to loud and obnoxious in two-point-five seconds flat.

"You know how it is, babe. The chicks all want a piece of this." He waved his hand up and down his body like some kind of a game show host. "Sometimes I prefer to travel incognito, you know?"

Oh, she knew, all right. Suppressing the twinge of disappointment, because she actually kinda liked the other guy more, Tracy nodded. "Yeah, I guess it would be hard having those... *babes* chasing you all the time." She turned her attention back to the male who held more appeal right now and rubbed his furry ears, smiling a little at his groan of delight. "You don't need to worry, I won't tell anyone you were here. I assume you came to say good-bye to your friend, Lucas Carmichael, and your sister?"

He paled and rose awkwardly, to pace a few feet away, his back ramrod straight under a soft looking dark blue cotton t-shirt. Even with the loose fit, Tracy could see the delineation of his muscular shoulders. Something clenched deep inside and it wasn't fear.

The faint cry of far off sirens told her that their time together was drawing to an end, but instead of relief, Tracy felt a keen sense of loss. Which was silly, she hardly knew the man, after all. But she couldn't deny her attraction and it didn't have anything to do with him being a movie star, as he'd intimated.

When Scott turned around his face was inscrutable, all emotion held under a tight wrap. "What do you know about Lucas?" he demanded.

She frowned at his tone, but then she thought about all the nosy reporters they'd been dealing with and realized it must be ten times worse on his end.

"I'm not a journalist, if that's what you're thinking."

He snorted at the polite term she'd used for the soul-stealing scavengers who made their living invading other people's privacy. They were unavoidable in his line of business—free publicity equals good publicity—but he hated feeling like a bug under a microscope. It wouldn't surprise him if they knew how often he took a shit, it was that bad.

She seemed too innocent to be a scum-sucker, but then, he'd been wrong before. This could all be some sort of elaborate set-up. The right time, and the right place, to catch him at his worst. He watched as she leaned forward to check on the dog again, her slim fingers running with practiced care over the animal's head and back. Her chestnut colored hair had fallen out of its topknot and now lay in wild disarray over her shoulders. She looked chilled. Her nipples were pressed against the white fabric of her blouse and a pink blush suffused her skin. Then again, that could be from his staring. He couldn't help himself; she was seriously hot in a sexy librarian meets rock star kind of way. Scott stifled the urge to wrap her in his arms and warm her from the inside out.

"Okay, say for half a minute I decided to take you at your word, tell me who you are then." He heard the whine of the sirens and swore under his breath. Their time together was quickly running out and this strange encounter would become a lost moment in his hectic life. He had the crazy urge to ask her to run away with him. Just disappear for a while, get to know one another, forget the past few years. Start over. Except that was impossible.

"Dr. Tracy York, a medical examiner. Your friend's accident is my case." She looked him in the eye, hers filled with compassion and he knew she was telling the truth.

Not a librarian then.

Reality came rushing back along with a truckload of pain and anger. Lucas was upstairs in a freaking vault, and here he was, making pansy eyes at a woman, the ME, no less. Self-disgust roiled in his gut and curdled his tone. "Fucking rights, it was an accident. That better be exactly what goes into the report too, Lucas deserves to rest in peace."

Her brows lowered and her mouth straightened into a tight line, pinching those full lips as though she'd tasted something sour. "Are you telling me to lie?"

His chin rose and his hand fisted at his side. "I'm *telling* you to do your job and let an innocent man have the farewell he deserves. That shouldn't be too hard, right?"

She could make an issue out of the open liquor in the car, even though Scott knew without a shred of doubt, Lucas was sober when he got behind that wheel. He'd only had a couple drinks all day.

The wail of the sirens almost drowned out her words, but the fire in her emerald eyes carried the message clearly. "I don't lie. *For anyone.*"

She would be one of the only women who didn't then.

"Is the guard going to know where to find you?" He lifted his voice to be heard, the noise reverberating off the cement walls now.

"What guard? There is no guard, it's a keyed entry."

Well, shit.

The man he'd met at the guardhouse must have been the attacker. And he'd let him go.

Chapter 6

Lucas sat in the cab across from the medical examiner's office and watched the ambulance screech to a halt at the entrance to the parking garage. Two patrol cars followed close behind. The flashing red and blue lights bounced off the walls as four officers jumped out of their vehicles and hurried forward, guns drawn. They waved the paramedics back until the guardhouse was cleared, then someone lifted the bar and the ambulance nosed its way through.

"Why didn't you stop him?"

The voice in the back jangled his already stretched nerves. He glared at the monk through the rear-view mirror. "You heard the rules as well as I did. No interfering with fate."

It had been tough enough to keep quiet when Scott asked him for a ride. He'd messed up when he called his old friend by the childhood nickname, A. Small wonder. No one knew of the names they had once called each other. It was their secret code, forged in the streets of their youth. Scott chose A for allegiance because it was the two of them, a team, against the craptastic world they inhabited. His was the more basic, T, for trustworthy. Yeah, he'd proven that was a wash, hadn't he?

"Well, if you're not going to do anything, let's get out of here." The monk leaned forward, his eyes filled with hope. "It's my turn. I want to see my family."

Lucas turned away from the man's pain and rubbed at his bristly chin. The Boss allowed them to enter the bodies of the living as long as they didn't change anything, but he'd kill for a shave. A frisson of electricity jolted his body as soon as the thought passed through his mind. He grunted and rode out the pain, his gaze on the now glowing cross hanging from the mirror.

"I didn't mean it literally, sheesh."

He rolled down the window and breathed in the moist loamy smell created by the timed sprinkler systems doing their job to keep the city green.

"What's your name, monk? We might as well try and get along. At least until the Boss decides I've done enough."

The guy snorted. "Done enough for what?" He tapped the back of the seat. "You think he's going to grant you a second chance or something? Oh, wait, I know. He'll bring you back as the injured dog. That would be fitting, wouldn't it?" He chuckled but there was no humor in the sound. "After all, it's because of drivers like you that I don't have my family."

Yeah, there was that.

The ambulance returned. With his new sense of perception, Lucas saw Scott sitting beside the woman from the lab in the rear of the vehicle. Their attention was centered on the animal laying tranquilized on the stretcher. A paramedic was checking vitals and setting a saline drip to stabilize the dog until they could get it to a veterinarian hospital.

"I don't get what He expects me to do. We aren't allowed to interfere, so why bring us down here?" His hand clenched the steering wheel as the ambulance sped past, carrying Scott away.

"You'll know when the time is right." The monk shifted restlessly. "Quit whining."

And on that pleasant note, Lucas started the car and shifted into gear. "You going to tell me how to get there, or do I need to guess?"

The monk's voice rattled like a snake. "One day, pretty-boy, you and I are going to seriously clash, and your ass will be mine."

"I didn't know you cared." Lucas grinned at the hiss from the backseat and pulled out onto the street, leaving the patrol cars behind. The sight of their flashing lights washed the smile from his lips. It had galled him to sit back and do nothing when that asshole escaped after wounding the mutt. The malevolence seeping from the man's mind had been disturbing. He'd seen his share of bullies and they all had the same thing in common—the will to hurt others weaker than themselves.

Natalya had fallen victim to their abuse more than once. He and Scott had made it their mission to protect her, especially as she grew older and the attention turned sexual in nature. Scott swore if anyone ever touched his little sister he'd kill them. Guess he didn't need to worry on that score any more.

Frustrated, Lucas drove his foot down hard on the gas pedal. The car screeched around the corner. A homeless man scurried out of the way, the headlights reflecting the whites of his eyes. The burn in Lucas' stomach turned into a raging inferno that rose up his esophagus and choked his breath. He slammed on the brakes, his heart triple-timing in his chest. A cold sweat broke out all over his body and turned his skin clammy.

"What the fuck, man?" The monk slammed his hand against the back of the seat, rattling Lucas's already jangled nerves.

Hadn't he learned anything from the accident? He could have killed that guy. His head fell forward and rested on top of the steering wheel, his breathing harsh in the strained silence.

Forgive me. Please—forgive me.

A soft breeze flowed through the open window, its warmth a blessing. Tears leaked from the corners of his eyes. He sniffed them back and sat up, his gaze meeting the accusing glare in the mirror.

"I'm sorry. It won't happen again." His voice was little more than a croak.

"Hmpf," the monk snorted. "Forgive me if I don't believe you." He shook his head in disgust. "Look, I don't like this any more than you do, but we're stuck with one another. Let's just make it work, okay? Preferably without you killing us a second time around."

Lucas swiped the moisture from his cheeks, and nodded. "Thanks," he muttered.

"Mike," the monk said. "The name is Mike."

Chapter 7

Scott couldn't believe he'd escaped from a hospital just a few hours before and now here he was, riding in the back of an ambulance. He was pretty sure it wasn't SOP to transport a canine, even if it was extenuating circumstances. But the moment the paramedics had shown up, his companion had run roughshod over their objections. It was sort of sexy.

Tracy York.

He had a difficult time equating her as a medical examiner. She seemed too… young. Naïve. Cute.

That is until a person got close enough to read the deep green pools of her gaze. They spoke of suffering, those eyes. They made him ache inside. He wanted to hold her. Offer to help, even though his world was a screwed up mess.

Her thigh rubbed against his every time the ambulance changed lanes and was slowly driving him crazy. Every nerve strained closer, waiting for the next teasing friction of silk and jean meshing together and then apart.

The vehicle took a corner and she lost balance, threw out a hand to steady herself, and came dangerously close to finding out exactly what she was doing to him.

Scott grasped her forearm in his good hand and stopped her forward momentum. He froze, their lips a hairsbreadth apart. Her eyes grew large and he felt like the wolf at Red Riding Hood's door. His heart skidded along his windpipe like it was an Olympic medal winning luge run. How had he thought her merely cute? She was gorgeous, with hair like the finest brandy and skin that rivalled any fairy tale heroine he'd ever read about. He leaned toward her, solely focused on tasting that lush, honey-sweet mouth.

And she frowned at him.

Just like that the noise came rushing back in, the creak of the van, the beep of machines, and the stifled snort of the paramedic who suddenly pretended to act busy. Tracy pulled her arm free. She ignored him to reach out and pet the mutt's gnarled coat, and move a careful few inches down the bench.

Scott glared at the grinning paramedic and sat back, his head resting against the cool metal wall behind him. He couldn't honestly remember the last time a woman turned him down. He was disappointed, but there was no denying the fact that the doc intrigued him. If she were anyone else he'd be tempted to pursue the matter. But she held his and Lucas' reputation in her dainty little hands. He couldn't afford to alienate her.

Tracy worked to slow her chaotic breathing, but her pulse was ping-ponging around her chest as though involved in a championship match. She threaded her fingers through the sleeping dog's thick coat and massaged, as much for her benefit as his, and tried to ignore Jenny smirking from her spot on the opposite seat. But then she'd seen Tracy shut down men's pick up lines before. The two women were part of an eclectic group who had first met at a book club and carried it over to Friday night bar hops. Not that any of them were drinkers—well, most of them weren't drinkers—they just enjoyed each other's company.

Tracy had the childish urge to stick her tongue out at her friend. She satisfied herself with a crinkled nose before lowering her gaze to the injured dog. She hoped Ken, the only male in their crowd, would be able to help the poor guy.

He'd almost kissed her.

Scott Anderson had almost laid those sexy movie star lips on her mouth. She was crazy to have turned him away. How many people could say they'd been kissed by Scott-freaking-Anderson?

Too many, and that was the problem. Tracy had no interest in seeing her name in the next gossip magazine—*Anderson's bro-mance ends in affair with M.E. -wonder what she's been inspecting?* After her sister's death, she'd developed an aversion to anything media related. The reporters made a gong show out of her family's distress. Nowadays, she seldom watched the news or read a paper, not that she was missing much—it was usually bad news anyway.

"So this is what you do in your off-time?" Jenny asked, her gaze mischievous as she eyed Scott over Tracy's shoulder.

Tracy glanced back, and was relieved to see his lids closed and his face slackening with sleep. He looked like he needed it too. Dark rings had made half-moon shadows under his eyes. His skin was pale and highlighted a string of fading bruises from his right cheek down to the edge of his collar. Sympathy that she knew he wouldn't appreciate, moved her to lift a blanket from the shelf and lay it over his lap. He shifted and she froze, her arms practically wrapped around him, her cheek inches from his chest. Then he settled and she sighed her relief.

She straightened on the hard bench and shrugged at Jenny's knowing smile. "He needs the rest."

Jenny snorted. "I just bet he does."

Tracy flushed. "It's not what you think. He was in an accident a few days ago and lost his sister and best friend."

Jenny's pretty face sobered. "Oh, that sucks." Then, it was like a light bulb came on. "Hey, I know who he is, the guys were talking about going out on that call. Heard it was a bad one. Head-on with a van, right?"

Tracy nodded. "Yeah, that's the one. The driver of the van didn't make it either. Left behind two kids and a pregnant wife who miscarried a few hours later."

Jenny swore. Working around a bunch of men every day gave her the vocabulary of a lumberjack. "They said alcohol was a factor. That bites. He deserved what he got then." Her gaze turned inflammatory on the unsuspecting Scott.

Tracy hurried to defend the sleeping man. "The investigation is ongoing. We don't know anything for sure yet, so give him the benefit of a doubt, okay?" She didn't know why she felt this sudden surge of protectiveness. She barely knew the man, but it was undeniable. He'd somehow managed to get under her skin.

The ambulance bounced over a speed bump and came to a stop. They had arrived. Jenny did another check of the pup's vitals, then prepared for transport.

Scott woke up with a start and groaned at the sudden movement. He gazed down at the blanket sliding off his legs and lifted a bemused stare in Tracy's direction.

She shrugged, self-conscious. "You looked cold."

They both reached for the fallen blanket at the same time and ended up bumping heads.

"Ouch." Tracy sat up and giggled, struck by the silliness of the situation.

Scott rose a bit slower, his hand cradling his chin. The poor man really was a mess.

"Are you okay?" he asked, the words a bit garbled.

"Me?" she laughed. "Look at you. There's not too many more places to get banged, are there?"

Almost before the words left her lips she wished them back. Scott looked surprised, then intrigued. Jenny hooted, and Tracy turned seven shades of red.

She flattened her hands to her overheated cheeks and refused to meet his eyes. "That's not, uh… yeah. I'll just stop now."

"Don't quit. People pay good money for this sort of entertainment." Jenny murmured, as she brushed past to open the rear doors.

There was no time to remain embarrassed. The driver met them at the back. They set the wheels down on the gurney and rolled toward the emergency entrance to the vet hospital. Scott climbed out and offered her a hand. Tracy hesitated, then grabbed on and the two of them hurried to catch the paramedics. Ken met them, smiled reassuringly, and began an assessment.

His practiced fingers ran over the animal's skull, withers, back and abdomen. He turned to them for a report, his gaze contemplating Scott's firm grip of her hand before he met her worried look with a quirk of his lips.

"When I asked you out on a date this wasn't what I had in mind," he teased.

Tracy stiffened, then realized what he was doing and raised her brows. Ken shrugged and turned his gaze to a now silent, Jenny.

"What do you have for me, Jen?"

Jenny thrust the clipboard into his arms. "Patient is stable. You can read the rest in my notes." She glanced at Tracy. "You okay now?" Tracy nodded, her chest hurting for her friend.

"C'mon, Dev, we better get back on shift." Jenny started toward the ambulance.

Dev gave Ken a commiserating look before hurrying after his departing partner.

Tracy shivered as she watched the lights fade away. Men. They really could be jerks sometimes.

She followed the gurney into the hospital, aware of Scott dogging her heels. The episode between Jenny and Ken couldn't have come at a better time. She knew better than to develop feelings for a guy. They couldn't be trusted. She'd make sure the pup was going to be okay and then she was going to say good-bye to Scott Anderson.

Chapter 8

T he shopping cart clattered its way down the sidewalk overloaded with an array of bottles, discarded clothing, scraps of pungent smelling food—and bells. It was those freaking *bells* that drove him onto the road in the first place. He'd already tried to remove them without success—they were tied with some kind of fisherman's knot even his knife couldn't cut—and so he'd been stuffing whatever he could find into them to dull the noise when the cart took off on him as though possessed.

With the cops just moments behind, Ray knew he couldn't just leave the blasted thing rolling down the street so he'd chased after it and almost ended up a shit-stain on the pavement when that cab rounded the corner.

He'd padded the shirt to increase his bulk, and with the addition of wide frame glasses and some face paint, even Anderson hadn't recognized him in that cheesy guard's uniform. But it wouldn't take long before every cop in the city would have a description and be hot on his trail, so he'd done what he needed to do. It wasn't that he enjoyed killing. It was simply a means to an end. That old bum looked like he was at death's door anyway. He'd just given him a push, that's all.

He grimaced over the odor of cheap wine and urine emanating from the filthy clothes, but beggars couldn't be choosers.

Ha. He snickered over his own joke. A few more blocks and he could ditch this flea-infested basket and get back to his own world. A world he'd worked hard to build up, and no one was going to take it away from him.

Lucas drove down the residential street at a snail's pace, his hands sweaty on the wheel. One yard had a trampoline sitting empty off to the side while in another a tire swing shaped like a pony swung from a big ol' willow tree.

"There." The newly named Mike pointed, his voice vibrating with suppressed emotion. "The one with the picket fence."

Of course it was.

Lucas guided the taxi into a parking space and killed the engine.

"I'll just wait here." He stared straight ahead and swallowed hard. "Take your time."

Silence descended like a dark shroud.

He slid the windows down and inhaled the sharp tang of night air along with the sweet, perfumed smell of Rugosa roses. His grandma had grown a set of matching bushes by her front door. One of few childhood memories he cared to remember.

The house was a perfect two-story white gingerbread with a wraparound porch and big bay windows for the parents to watch their children at play.

Except, now there was only one parent.

Two kids' bikes lay discarded in the driveway and the grass was in need of a mow. A single light shone from inside, as if the rest of the home lay steeped in sorrow and sadness.

A figure appeared on the doorstep and Lucas tensed. "Who's…?" He glanced in the rear of the car, the words dying off when he realized he was alone. That was going to take some getting used to. He turned back in time to see Mike just sort of glide through the closed door. Lucas blinked hard and shook his head, stunned.

"Don't be so surprised. We angels have many gifts in our arsenal." The rich baritone of the Lord's voice resonated throughout the car. Lucas froze, his gaze going to the radio softly glowing even though the vehicle was still turned off.

"You trying to give me a heart attack?" he demanded.

"It's a bit late for you to worry about your human body, I'd think," the voice replied.

Great, now he had a smart-assed car to deal with.

You know better than that.

Chastised, Lucas dropped his head. His attitude always managed to get him in trouble, especially in times of stress, and this whole situation definitely qualified in his top ten.

"I meant no disrespect."

The lights flickered from the radio. "I understand, my son. It takes time to get a handle on this new world you inhabit. Just remember, we are not the enemy."

No, that honor was reserved for himself. He'd always been his own worst enemy.

"Stop feeling sorry for yourself. Your focus should be on helping others, not on needless self-pity."

Lucas' cheeks heated. He opened his mouth to deny the condemnation, then let it slide shut. The man was right. It was too late to change what he'd done. All he could do was try and help those he'd hurt.

The second story window slid open. A head peeked out before disappearing from view to be replaced by a set of pajama-clad legs. The child sat on the sill, then suddenly without warning lunged, stopping Lucas' heart until the small arms grasped the nearby branch of an old oak tree.

Without conscious thought, he flew to the base of the tree and prepared to catch the slight body if he should fall, but the boy was a monkey. He swung from branch to branch as if he'd been doing so all his life. When he got close to the ground, he let himself just hang there until his hands couldn't take the weight any longer. He dropped to the grass with a soft grunt and sat there for a moment, then he stood, dusted the butt of his dinosaur pj's, and searched until he found the pack he'd let go of in his descent. He shouldered it and turned to head down the driveway and that's when Lucas saw the tears.

Aw, shit.

The kid was running away.

Lucas needed to do something, like now.

He picked up a fallen acorn, threw it toward the rose bushes he'd been admiring earlier and hoped it would freak the child out and send him back inside where he'd be safe. Instead the boy turned white, jumped like he'd been struck by lightning, and bolted down the street.

Good job, moron.

He ran, but the kid was fast, especially now with Lucas' new, less than healthy body, and it wasn't long before he lost sight of him. He slowed down for a minute, straining to catch the sound of retreating steps over his sawing breaths, but there was nothing. He swore and glanced back, but the car was silent. Obviously this was up to him to handle.

He bundled his jacket around a sagging middle and continued down the road, stopping every so often to listen. Where did the kid go? There were numerous hiding spots; hedges, garbage cans, sheds, cars. It was the latter that kept Lucas searching. The kid was wearing dark clothing; he wouldn't have a chance if a car came along at the wrong moment.

Please. Show me a sign.

The silent plea paid off. A faint crash and cry of pain gave him an answer. Lucas broke into a running walk, all the while praying for the child's safety.

Agony unlike anything he'd ever endured ripped through his body, driving him onto his hands and knees. The pain was so intense he barely felt the pebbles gouging his skin. The next wave when it came left him weak and shaking, on the edge of passing out. He breathed through the ache and fought to rise, worry for the child driving him forward. There was a sudden shift of air and he was on his feet and rocking, counterbalanced by a huge weight on his back. Stunned, Lucas twisted and his eyes went wide.

A magnificent set of swan-like wings rose from his shoulder blades. Their span had to be nearly eight feet in width, each feather snowy white. His pulse jumping crazily he tried an experimental flap. His feet lifted off the ground, then dropped him none too gently back to earth.

Holy shit.

He'd been kidding the other day when he asked for wings. This was nuts. Talk about your roller coaster rides. His gut hadn't caught up to the last changes, now these… wings. He had freaking wings.

Another cry from the next street over and with the slightest direction his wings unfurled and guided him over the rooftops to a view that froze his blood.

The kid lay trapped on his side against an old wooden shed while a bunch of teens took turns kicking him as though he were a soccer ball and they were looking to make a goal.

Lucas let loose a hair-raising screech and dove, anger a deep burn in his chest. The group on the ground looked up, and stark fear took hold of their features. He knew all about bullies and planned on teaching them a lesson they wouldn't soon forget.

He landed on the balls of his feet between Mike's son and the teens and only stumbled a little this time. He allowed a quick glance to make sure the kid was okay and widened his stance, folding his arms, which seemed to have grown some impressive pipes, over his now solid chest.

This is more like it.

One of the teens, a punker with scraped back green-tinged hair and a ring through his nose, spat near Lucas' kickass biker boots.

"Halloween isn't for a couple weeks yet, old man."

Old. Ha. Little did he know.

"Back off," he warned. "You boys are treading dangerous ground. One bad mistake can screw up your whole lives. You don't want to do that, do you?"

The other two looked suitably chastised and hung their heads. But the pack leader wasn't willing to back down. He grabbed a nearby piece of pipe and brandished it in the air as though he were a modern day *Peter Pan*.

Aware that he couldn't change the boy's free will, Lucas decided to try out his newfound powers. He closed his eyes and a lift of his hand later, the teen wore neon tights to match that awful hair color. His friends broke out in guffaws of choked laughter.

The teen glared at Lucas. "Funny, dude. I don't know how you pulled it off, but this ain't over."

He turned and marched off into the night, his butt a beacon in the dark. His friends followed, snickering.

Now that he'd taken care of the problem, Lucas turned to help Mike's boy.

But the kid was gone.

Chapter 9

The coffee they served in the waiting room of the veterinary hospital could have been used to sterilize the equipment. Tracy inspected her spoon, shrugged, and added another cube of sugar to the mix. She had a feeling she was going to need the boost.

She wandered the confines of the room, careful to avoid the corner where Scott was chitchatting with the nurse who had taken their information. Far be it for her to care about the fact the woman was practically sitting in his lap. Or that her breasts were mashed against his arm. And how could he stand her gigglitis condition?

Tracy leaned a tired shoulder against the window frame and stared into the darkness beyond. A hot bath, a glass of red wine, and her warm bed sounded like a slice of heaven. The events of the day were catching up to her. She could feel her hard-won poise deflating by the second.

Ken had assured her the pup would be fine. In fact, he'd told her to go home and he'd call in the morning, but she and the animal had connected in the garage. Tracy couldn't leave without making sure he pulled through. This case had her worried. Their team had performed autopsies in the past on everything from high-ranking officials to gang members and sometimes even received hate mail. This was different. Malicious.

"Penny for them?" Scott's reflection joined hers in the glass, his voice a velvet cloak wrapping her in his sensuality.

More than anything Tracy wanted to lean back against his broad chest, feel his strong arms hug her close, and just relax. She couldn't. Too many years of managing on her own had programmed her not to count on anyone. If only her hormones didn't respond so easily to his oh-so-delicious body.

Because that's all this was, a chemistry attraction. It had to be. They barely knew each other. And he was a player. All solid reasons to take what she wanted and walk away. Problem was, Tracy wasn't sure she could walk away from this man.

Scott barely listened to the young nurse perched beside him on the hard plastic chairs, buzzing in his ear like an annoying mosquito. Tracy seemed pensive and alone standing by the window. He ached to hold her close. They had a connection; she might wish to deny it but it was there just the same.

He should take her home. She needed to get some rest before the cops showed up to take their statements. He'd tried calling Ray to do some damage control but his PR manager wasn't picking up the phone. Damn guy was always around when he wasn't wanted and never when he was needed. The same thing happened the night of the party.

He and Lucas had spent the day sightseeing, showing his little sister the city of Chicago. They began with a boat tour on the Chicago River, checked out the Ferris wheel at Navy Pier, and ended with a stroll around Buckingham Fountain in Grant Park. Then they'd gone home and dressed in preparation for the after-party now that the movie had wrapped up production.

Ray promised to have a car deliver them to the gathering hosted by the movie's director, but Lucas decided to go for a cruise and show Natalya some of the area surrounding the city first. He'd just bought a sweet ride a couple of weeks earlier and was still in car whore heaven. They had a blast, laughing and singing and catching up with each other. Idyllic really.

Restless, he smiled vaguely in his companion's direction, rose and made his way across the empty sitting room to stand slightly behind Tracy. He inhaled the flowery scent of her shampoo, tempted to bury his nose in the silky tresses. How could she still look so put together after the day they'd just endured? Her hair, almost mahogany in this lighting, hadn't dared to escape its coiled perfection. Even her clothes were wrinkle-free, though dusty from kneeling on the cement.

He itched to mess her up. To find out what she'd look like first thing in the morning, after a full night of lovemaking. He'd start with the tender spot right there on the back of her neck, work his way to the shell of her ear. Murmur how beautiful she looked, how much he wanted her, how great they were going to be together. He'd remove the pins and work his fingers through the silky mass of hair, cradle her head while his teeth nibbled her jaw and inched closer and closer to the pouty fullness of her mouth. He fantasized about that mouth—and what it could do to him.

She would be fully responsive, as eager to learn his body as he was to discovering hers. She'd turn to him, run her slender hands up his chest, unbutton his shirt and touch his skin. Her lush lips would trail fire along his collarbone, nuzzle his neck, and then her mouth would lift to his and whisper for him to take her home with him.

Yeah, maybe.

It was far more likely that if she knew what he was thinking she'd push him out the third story window of the hospital.

"Did you get her number?" Tracy glanced back, her brow raised over sarcastic green eyes.

Wow, someone's claws were out. Never mind that she was right. The nurse, Nancy, he thought she'd said, had given him her card. And asked for an autograph on her tit. Cripes, was she going to whip the thing out every time she wanted to show off his signature? Scott didn't understand what drove mega-fans to act the way they did. Some of it was just plain creepy.

He fingered the crumpled card in his pocket.

"Nah, not interested." Funny thing, he really wasn't. Even though Nurse Nancy would most certainly have been a sure thing, he had his eye on someone else entirely. And Tracy wasn't even his type. Normally he sought out cardboard blondes who knew the score every bit as much as he did. Tracy reminded him more of an owl, with her still air and eyes that saw everything. Yet when she soared Scott bet it would be breathtaking. He planned to be the one to find out.

"I'm fine here. Ken can give me a ride home later."

Not on your life, sister.

He wasn't leaving the door open for that guy to step in. "Let me take you."

Her gaze grew wary. Smart girl.

He used his good hand and eased the now cold coffee from her grip, turned and set it on the table next to the wall, then gestured for her to lead the way.

"C'mon, you're dead on your feet. We'll stop at the front desk and give them a number to call in case of emergencies. I'm sure your friend will take good care of the pup, right?" An unexpected surge of protectiveness moved him to place his hand at the small of her back to guide her down the hall. She fit neatly under his arm, a Pocket Venus, the top of her head barely brushing his chin. Voluptuous, curvy, and soon to be his.

He was thankful when they stopped at the admission's desk and neither Nurse Nancy nor Doc Ken were anywhere in sight. A moment later they were out the door and into the cab he'd called earlier. She gave him an impenetrable glance, then leaned forward and gave the driver her address before settling back in the seat, hands folded primly in her lap.

She smelled even better in the close confines of the dark car. His body tightened. He gave up maintaining a friendly distance and let his thigh rub against hers while his arm snaked around her shoulders. His lips brushed her forehead. When she didn't immediately move away he obeyed the urge and moved lower; skimming her eyelid, discovering the smooth, clean line of her cheekbone, the silky texture of her skin. And then he was where he wanted to be, his mouth tasting her lips.

His heart was pounding like a teenager's, for fuck's sake. His hands were trembling and he was sweating. Crazy. He couldn't remember the last time a woman had affected him this way. He nibbled the corner of her mouth, seeking permission to enter. Her lips quivered. Then, thank you sweet baby Jesus, they opened on a soft sigh of acceptance.

Scott used the fingers resting on her shoulder to gently nudge her jaw, turning her so they could fit together more fully. She flicked out her tongue to catch his lower lip and his dick jumped in reaction.

Holy hell.

He was in so much trouble.

Now that she was fully on board, her hands and mouth were everywhere at once. Her taste was indescribable. Like his favorite dark chocolate black forest cake, sweet, rich, decadent, and he couldn't get enough. Their tongues mated in a way he craved for their bodies to match. He strained closer, frustrated that with his broken arm he couldn't touch her the way he desired.

Her hand skimmed down his side and brushed against his cracked rib. Scott sucked in a harsh breath and couldn't withhold a groan of pain. Tracy jumped as though she'd been scalded, unintentionally bumping him again.

"Oh," she gasped. "I'm so sorry. Are you okay?"

That depends. Did she plan on continuing where they left off?

Scott eyed her horrified expression and sighed. *Yeah, thought not.*

"Sure," he grimaced and surreptitiously straightened a leg to ease the pressure. "I'm good." He caught the cabbie's amused gaze in the mirror and used his knee to shove a warning through the back of the seat. He didn't care for himself, but it seriously pissed him off at the thought of Tracy's humiliation. He knew better than this. They'd be lucky if their kiss wasn't turned into a sordid affair on the front cover of a celebrity site by morning.

She inched away, smoothing her mussed hair back into its neat twist. He smothered his dissatisfaction and slumped in his seat. Just as well, he wasn't in the right headspace to be screwing around with anyone right now, especially a woman like Tracy.

Raise a little hell sang from his cell phone. Tracy's eyebrows rose. He exhaled and dug into his pocket for the blasted thing.

"Tracy, hi, it's Ken."

Scott fingered the end button, caught Tracy's enquiring gaze, and reluctantly passed the phone over.

She listened for a moment, then turned away for privacy. Scott forced himself to stay in his corner, his ears straining to eavesdrop.

"How is he?" Tracy asked. She cleared her throat, her voice husky. Scott's chest filled with satisfaction. He got to her.

The doc must have shared some good news, her posture eased. "Thanks, Ken, I owe you one."

She ended the call just as the cab pulled up in front of a set of brownstone type condos. "I have to go. I'll see you then."

She gave Scott a small non-smile, handed his cell back, and dug in her purse, obviously intending to pay the cabdriver and blow him off.

He reached out and stilled her movements.

"The pup's okay?" When she nodded, he sighed his relief. "Good, that's really good." Reluctant to end the night alone he gently squeezed her fingers. "You going to invite me in?"

The moment the words left his lips he wished them back. Her hand stiffened, withdrew from under his, and came out with a wad of cash that she passed to the waiting cabbie. Then she finally met his gaze, her chin lifting proudly.

"I don't think that's a good idea, do you?"

Yeah, he really did.

He watched as she opened the door and climbed out, revealing a length of shapely thigh in the process.

When she leaned over enough to see him, her face seemed a touch wistful. "Take care of yourself, Scott."

Before he could answer, she softly closed the door and walked off into the night.

Chapter 10

Lucas grabbed his chest, wheezing like a two-pack-a-day truck driver with asthma by the time he walked back to the car. Apparently this new superhero persona only worked in an emergency. Would a heart attack count?

Shivering, he climbed behind the wheel and started the engine before directing the heat vents to high. He still couldn't believe he had wings. Talk about your kickass movie prop. This would almost be fun if it weren't for the fact the kid was wandering around out there in nothing more than a pair of cotton pajamas. He needed to find him, and soon. Lucas dreaded telling Mike he'd allowed his child to go missing, the guy was in enough pain. Maybe if he toured the neighborhood he could catch a break and locate the little fella.

Decision made, Lucas shifted into gear and idled away from the curb before clicking on his headlights. At the corner he hung a right, heading in the same general direction of where he'd last seen the boy. The kid would be alright, he had to be. He was probably holed up in someone's garden shed or garage and would head for home in the morning. But Lucas didn't want to wait that long. He didn't much like Mike, but the man deserved to know his family was safe.

It was because of someone like him that Mike was in heaven. If only he'd been paying more attention to the road that day. But no, he hadn't been able to keep his gaze from straying to his buddy's kid sister. Scott's fully grown, incredibly gorgeous, younger sibling who managed to fill the car with her captivating presence. Where had the mouthy little pig-tailed squirt who used to follow them all over the neighborhood disappear to? This older, poised version of Natalya was worlds apart from that little girl. Or so it seemed—until he looked closer and noticed the mischievous sparkle in her teal blue eyes, and the errant curl of sandy blonde hair that refused to stay tucked behind the delicate pink shell of her ear. She'd worn a white dress. It should have looked prim and proper with its scooped neck and demure hem, but instead fit her like a second skin.

Lucas had been flat-out gob-smacked. He'd known she was a pretty girl, he and Scott had had their hands full keeping the dickheads away from her when they were younger, but this… She'd gone and grown up on him when he wasn't looking and he wasn't sure what to do with all the heat surging in his belly—and lower.

Shit.

She was his best friend's sister, and by extension, his. It was plain wrong to be wondering if those breasts were as firm as they looked, how smooth those long, long legs of hers were, or how they would feel wrapped around his waist.

She'd asked him to hold her beer while she shifted to get more comfortable on Scott's lap. Lucas felt like an idiot because he'd gone and bought a two-seater dream-machine instead of something practical. He remembered raising the drink in a toast and taking a light sip, his focus on Nat instead of the freaking road. When he'd turned back his vision was blurry and it was already fait accompli, far too late to save anybody. Natalya was dead, just like Mike's family who had lost their husband and father.

"It's time you stopped feeling sorry for yourself. It's unproductive and will do you no good."

Lucas swerved, startled out of his thoughts by the chastising tone of his Lord. "Don't do that," he swore. "One accident in a lifetime is more than enough."

Anger settled like an oppressive cloud on his chest and choked the peacefulness of the night sky from his mind.

"Why are you doing this?" He slapped the steering wheel in frustration. "I couldn't even protect my friends and now you want me to rescue a kid?" He slammed the car into park.

"Find some other saint to do your saving. I quit."

The Lord chuckled. "You're just like your grandfather, he's always sassing me, too."

Stunned, Lucas glanced around, but the back seat was still empty. "You know my grandpa?" Of course, he'd know everyone.

"I do, my son. He's a good man. Hot tempered, but a good man nonetheless."

Visions of a jovial smile and gentle hands filled Lucas' mind superseded by images of coarse swearing and fists the size of ham hocks. When he'd been small his grandfather was his whole world. Always kind and sympathetic to a little boy's scuffed knees or dirty hands. But then he'd died and left them alone and nothing was ever the same again.

"I want to see him," Lucas said, his gaze on the golden cross.

"And you will. In time," He replied. "First, you have work to do."

Scott watched until Tracy made it safely into the building, disgusted with himself for making a stupid play on a woman who obviously wasn't a player. He'd never met anyone quite like the doc before. It surprised him how much her opinion mattered in such a short space of time. And it pissed him off that she didn't take him seriously. Maybe he wasn't a high-falutin' vet like ol' Ken, but his career choice was no walk in the park either. He spent endless hours studying and repeating phrases over and over again, then there were the wardrobe changes, makeup, extreme heat, or freezing cold. Kissing and sometimes more with women he'd barely met, and frankly, couldn't care less about. Months of exhausting travel and promotion followed by a never-ending rinse and repeat cycle.

Maybe he was becoming jaded. The life he and Lucas led was disturbingly shallow when placed against the importance of Tracy's occupation. No wonder she brushed him off. He'd have done the same in her position.

"Where to, mister?"

The cabbie's voice roused him from his musings. He slouched back in his seat, wincing at the growing ache in his side. He'd overdone it for his first day out of the hospital.

His cell beeped and he fumbled in his haste to retrieve the phone from his pocket. Maybe she'd changed her mind. The name lit up on the screen put paid to those fantasies. It was only his agent. He fingered the call button but couldn't bring himself to press it. Ray was a good guy, but he had no conscience. It was all about the next big film with the man. Usually Scott didn't mind because that was his goal also—but not any more.

"You know any good parks around here?" He silenced the ringer and slid it back into his pocket.

"Yeah, sure. There's a fairly quiet one just a few blocks from here, but you better be careful, mate. You make an easy mark looking like that," the cabbie said.

Scott shrugged. He'd welcome a good fight. Maybe it would relieve some of the God-awful tension he'd been under since the crash.

"Whatever, man, it's your dime." The driver shifted into gear and Scott took a last look at the brownstone swiftly disappearing from view.

Ten minutes later he'd paid the cabbie and exited into the quiet sanctuary of the park. There were enough lights interspersed along the walkway to push back the enveloping darkness but not so many that he felt like he was on stage. This was good, better than a night of meaningless sex with a woman he barely knew.

Yeah, sure. Keep telling yourself that.

The further he gimped along the path and worked out the kinks, the looser his muscles became. He'd taken the painkillers Nurse Ratchet left on the bedside table before he vacated the hospital. Tomorrow he'd call and see about getting a prescription for more, though he had a huge aversion to drugs of any kind. Too many of his buddies had gone down that path and never escaped.

The trail led to a gazebo on a little rise in the center of an open area. Scott glanced around, but all was silent. Even the fickle breeze had died down. Hundreds of twinkling lights lit up a midnight blue sky, and though he searched, there were no falling stars. Too bad, he could use a wish about now.

He strode up the path to the entrance of the gazebo, squinting to make out the shapes of a couple of benches. A sturdy wicker chair beckoned. He made his way into the dark building, tested the seat for dryness, and sank down with a sigh of relief. After almost a week in the hospital his energy level was low and it hadn't been the easiest of nights. If Lucas were here he'd tell him to quit acting like a pussy and grab a set. And Natalya would be fussing over him like a mother hen. His fists clenched and he squeezed his eyes shut against the tsunami of grief threatening to drag him under. What was he going to do without them?

A noise woke him and his free hand went to the base of his neck to massage away the kinks from his awkward position. He must have dozed off. The shuffling sound came again from off to his right. Scott swore and straightened up.

Brilliant, Einstein.

He'd be lucky if he didn't get rolled.

"Who's there?"

The sudden silence grew even more oppressive. He rose, careful not to betray any weakness to his, as yet, unseen opponent, even though his side was on fire from sitting too long. A glimmer of white gave the other guy's position away. Scott moved as unobtrusively as he could to place the heavy wicker chair between them as a sort of bulwark.

"Look, I don't have much cash but you can take what's here." He pulled his wallet free and flung a few dollars down on the seat. "Here. Take it." He tensed, preparing to protect himself against an attack.

The white moved up and down and the air stirred with the unmistakable sound of wings.

What the…? His pulse kicked up a gear and his hands grew clammy.

An apparition stepped forward into a patch of moonlight and Scott's mouth dropped open.

"Hey, buddy."

Lucas stood before him with a crooked grin and a huge motherfuckin' set of wings on his back.

Chapter 11

Michael Crenshaw stood inside the door of his home, closed his eyes, and just breathed. He could still smell the bubblegum scent that always clung to his youngest son's skin. He even fancied he could hear his oldest boy giggling as Mike threw him over his shoulder and swung him around after returning from a hard day's work. He could see his wife's sweet smile as she hurried from the kitchen. Taste her cherry red lips as she stood on her toes to kiss him hello.

God, he missed them.

The full force of all he'd lost hit him.

Why? Why did this happen to him? What had he done so wrong? The ache intensified until he couldn't bear it and fell to his knees, head bowed in pain and sorrow.

Julie's sobbing broke through his misery some time later and brought him to his feet. It came from their bedroom. He made his way down the hall, his steps dragging as dread took over. Jules lay curled up on the bed, her arms wrapped tight around a chocolate brown teddy bear. The crib the two of them had been building together before the crash lay in a jumbled heap of kindling in the center of the floor. She'd destroyed it.

He stumbled across the room, his hands trembling to hold her. To offer comfort. *Oh, Jules.* He'd been so busy worrying about everything he'd lost, he hadn't taken into account his wife's agony. Her crying had disintegrated into the occasional hiccup and sniffle as exhaustion claimed her body. She'd lost weight since the accident. Her cheeks were hollowed, her hair lackluster.

They'd just learned they were expecting a baby girl and it was hard to say who was more excited; him and Julie, or the boys. They'd been laughing and talking, making up names, each sillier than the one before. Mike remembered turning his head for a split second to tease Dustin over his choice, Thumbelina, when Julie cried out a warning. He'd taken one glance at her horrified face and *known* they were in trouble. The rest was a blur; a little convertible sports car barreling right for them, his fingers slipping as he tried to avoid a head-on collision. The kids screaming in his ear as they picked up on the sudden tension and Jules turning to use her body as a barrier to try and save the boys, tears streaming down her face as she chanted, "I love you, I love you, I love…"

He didn't get the chance to say good-bye.

They'd had eight tumultuous, perfect years together. Not enough, not even close. And now because some jackass drove into them he'd never get the chance to see his boys grow up. Walk his daughter down the aisle. Or grow old with the woman he loved more than all the angels in heaven. His gaze went to the wrecked crib and hatred flared hot and dangerous.

Someone was going to pay.

Scott swayed and made a grab for the chair before he did a face plant in front of… of whatever it was standing across the room. A hallucination from the drugs, had to be.

"Bet you never thought you'd be seeing my ugly mug again, did ya?" the apparition asked.

It sounded like his friend. It even looked like Lucas—well, except for the wings. He sealed his eyes shut, but when they re-opened, it was still there sporting a goofy grin.

Maybe he'd hit his head harder than he thought.

"Are ya goin' to say something?" The creature took a step forward, into the glow from the moon, and Scott sucked in an awed breath. He was beautiful. His iridescent wings folded gracefully against his back creating a frame for his all-too-familiar head. His body was more defined—muscular, like Lucas on steroids. And where the old Lucas preferred dress slacks and shiny shoes, this one wore worn jeans and biker boots.

"I don't believe this," Scott whispered, his head shaking violently in denial.

The creature chuckled. "I know, right? Freaking crazy. Me, an angel."

Well, at least they were in agreement.

"How? Why?" Scott couldn't articulate what was going through his head right now. How could this be possible? It wasn't that he didn't believe in a hereafter—but angels? Even stranger—*Lucas* as an angel?

The spirit moved nearer and Scott could see the worry etched on his friend's face as he stared at him. "You better sit down, buddy, you're looking pretty pale."

No kidding.

Seeing a ghost tended to do that to a guy.

Scott sidestepped the chair to get a closer look. If he was hallucinating, this was one hell of a dream. He stretched out an unsteady hand and brushed a downy feather, the color of a cotton ball. He looked up and met the hazel gaze he knew as well as his own.

"You're real." A hard ball of emotion choked him. Tears leaked down his face. Overwhelmed, he wrapped his arm around Lucas' neck and dragged him close. "I can't believe it. You're here."

Warm breath whispered near his ear. "I'm so fricken sorry, Scott. So sorry." Lucas' arms hugged him back, pinching his ribs, but he didn't care. He wasn't alone anymore.

"Well isn't this sweet?" A voice snickered, and laughter from others followed.

Lucas stiffened. His arms tightened, smothering Scott, before he stepped away, placing himself in front of the newcomers. Scott was left staring at a six-foot wing span.

The room got deadly quiet.

"Figured you wouldn't take my advice," Lucas drawled, the words deceptive. His body prepared for attack, from legs spread wide to thick shoulders and fists the size of cement blocks hanging by his side.

What was he talking about? Who were these guys?

The questions would have to wait. For now he needed to stand with his friend and try to be a help instead of a hindrance. He glanced around for some kind of weapon and noticed a broom leaning against the wall; it would have to do.

He grabbed the handle and moved to Lucas's left so his good arm was free to swing. He could see three, maybe four, teenagers, and by the scent of the wacky tobbaccy they were passing around, they were partying down. He didn't care, they could just take it down the road. This was his haven for the moment.

Scott figured he'd try the friendly approach first. "Hey, how's it going?"

Did teens even say that any more? He shrugged and took a few steps toward their leader, a kid with spiked green hair. Lucas hissed a warning behind him that he chose to ignore. "Look, we were here first. Why don't you and your buddies find a new place to hang out?"

The punker eyed him up and down, then blew a ring of smoke in his face. "Why don't you make us?" He pulled a hand out of his pocket and made his point with the business end of a switchblade.

Lucas snarled.

One of the other kids swore and dropped a beer, the yeasty smell vaporizing on the crisp night air. "C'mon man, let's get outta here."

The Punker ignored him and flopped into Scott's recently vacated chair. "You guys tellin' me you're scared of a couple of gimped up weirdoes? Cut me a break."

Pot, meet kettle.

Scott sighed. Obviously this kid was spoiling for a fight. Too bad he wasn't up to granting him his wish. "Whatever, dude. Knock yourself out."

He turned away, motioning for Lucas to precede him out the door. It wasn't worth the hassle.

The chair scraped the floor. Before he could swing around to see what happened, Lucas slammed him to the ground. The air whooshed from his lungs as his friend's six foot plus frame impacted with his already bruised body. Lucas' wings encompassed them, creating a shield. Scott heard shouting and feet pounding as the teens ran away.

"'kay, we're clear. Let me up, you're squishing me." He used his free hand to lever it under Lucas' shoulder. He wasn't moving.

"C'mon, buddy, let me up." Desperation crept into his voice. Something was wrong. He pushed harder and finally managed to roll Lucas onto his side.

Scott sat up, cradling his side. Lucas' eyes were closed and his skin looked white with shock. What the hell happened?

The wings folded and disappeared into his back and Scott's eyes pulled a *Roger Rabbit.*

Holy shit.

His friend's brown hair changed color, going almost gray and bristly. Even his body shape and clothing changed, developing a middle-aged paunch covered by a stained T-shirt and green cargo pants.

Scott scooted awkwardly backward on the floor, his heart jolting in disbelief. It was the cab driver who'd picked him up at the hospital. This was too freaking weird for words.

"What the hell is going on?" He wiped a shaking hand across his mouth and wished he'd taken the kid up on a toke.

A stain had widened on Lucas' side. Scott inched closer, grabbing the discarded broom handle on his way. He lightly touched the stain and brought his fingers to his nose. The coppery scent of blood filled his nostrils.

"Shit." He glanced around wildly, searching for his phone. A glint caught his eye and he jumped to his feet, ignoring his own screaming muscles, and hurried to the edge of the bench. He used the broom to sweep the object out where he could grab it. It was his cell, thank God.

He thumbed it open and was about to dial emergency when Lucas cried out, "No, don't."

He sat up slowly, cradling his side. "I'm fine."

"You're *not* fine. Even without the fact that you sprouted tail feathers and you're supposed to be freakin *dead,"* Scott swore and exhaled a harsh breath. "Someone stabbed you, man. You need to get some help."

Lucas/cabbie guy grimaced, his cheeks now resembling rosy red apples. He gingerly tugged the material away from the wound and lifted his shirt for a better look, revealing an ugly red gash along the ribcage.

"It's not that bad, just a slice. It'll heal." He tugged the shirt over his head and plastered it against the cut.

Scott wasn't so sure. Even if the injury wasn't as bad as he thought, that shirt was bound to invite infection. It was beyond strange hearing his best friend's voice coming from the middle-aged man sitting on the ground. They made a great pair, both of them dinged up and a little worse for wear. Well, except for the fact that Lucas wasn't real. This would make a great script. He snorted, imagining his publicist's face if he suggested such a crazy concept. They'd lock him up and throw away the key.

He carefully lowered himself beside the other man, choking back a groan from the fresh bruises he sported thanks to Lucas' earlier imitation of a linebacker.

"Let me see."

Lucas glared but dropped the cloth. Scott turned on the phone's flashlight and winced at the angry looking tear in the man's skin.

"Well, doc? Am I going to live?"

"Really? That the best you can come up with?" Scott slapped the cloth back into place and smirked at Lucas' pained groan.

"You should work on your bedside manner," Lucas grunted. "It sucks, dude."

Scott swallowed hard. That was such a Lucas thing to say.

"It really is you, isn't it?"

"I've been telling you that." Lucas shivered against the October chill.

Scott dragged his coat off his good arm and passed it across. "Put this on before you catch your death."

Lucas croaked out a laugh and Scott grinned in return. It was bittersweet to have his buddy back again.

Chapter 12

Tracy spent a sleepless night and rose while dawn was still little more than a glimmer in the sky. She went through the motions of her yoga routine, a quick shower, and a cup of instant coffee, then strode briskly in the early morning chill to the bus stop. It would be good to get her car back. It's not that she minded the bus, but preferred time to wake up before she was thrown into the hectic pace of the city. At least in her car she had a bubble between her and the next guy. On the bus there was no such luxury—as an overweight woman packing a suitcase for a purse and smelling like cheap perfume proved by taking up three-quarters of the seat beside her.

She tugged her cell phone out of the pocket squished between them, ignoring the woman's indignant huff, and called the veterinary hospital to check on Sugar-Bear. Sometime during their misadventure last night the name had popped into her head for the poor thing. He was lucky, his injuries could have been much worse. She'd interrupted whatever was about to happen and she was grateful Scott had come on the scene when he had. Not enough to sleep with him, but grateful nonetheless.

Though, holy toledo, the man could kiss.

Her toes curled in her black pumps just thinking about that sexy mouth and where she wanted it the most. The receptionist picked up the call and Tracy forced her thoughts back to the hapless mutt.

"Can you connect me with Dr. Foster, please?"

"One moment and I'll check if he's in." The nurse placed her on hold and soft elevator music streamed into her ear along with the annoying crinkling of paper coming from the woman beside her.

Tracy glanced sideways and was astounded to see what seemed like a seven course meal courtesy of a fast food restaurant emerge from the enormous handbag. The lady noticed her look and offered half a bagel slathered in cream cheese. Tracy leaned back in her seat and tipped her coffee cup in reply. The woman shrugged and lifted the bagel to her mouth, sighing with pleasure.

Tracy shuddered and turned back to the window.

"Hello?" A tinny voice reminded her that she'd let the phone drop to her lap.

She hurried to place it to her ear. "Ken?"

"Tracy, I was hoping to hear from you." His voice was cheerful.

The tension she'd been holding on her shoulders fell away. "He's going to be fine then?" She stared at the shop fronts racing by the window, the streets teaming with people heading to work.

"I expect a full recovery, yes. You can come and pick him up later today, how's that sound?"

Great, it sounded great, except for the part of her picking him up. She hadn't thought that far ahead. What was she going to do with a dog? Tracy cringed at the thought of turning him over to the pound, though that was probably his best chance. But they always looked so sad in those cages when the animal shelters ran fund-raising commercials. It felt cruel to even contemplate the pound for Sugar-Bear after everything he'd been through. Maybe she could keep him at her place for now—just until she could find him a good home.

"Great, thanks Ken. I'll stop by after work."

"Not so fast. You owe me one, remember?" Ken teased, laughter in his voice. "How about I bring him with me and meet you at your place for a coffee and I can drop off this week's book since you missed book club?"

Shoot, she'd forgotten. She hadn't even started last week's reading assignment yet.

"Rain check? And Ken?" Tracy smiled. "Thanks."

She clicked the phone shut and tucked it away, already planning to stop at the pet store on her lunch break. After all, Sugar-Bear would need food and a bed. Maybe some toys.

"That your young man?" her seat-mate asked.

Tracy straightened her jacket along her back. "No, just a friend."

Funny how a picture of Scott Anderson popped into her head at the woman's words. She'd hurt him last night though she hadn't meant to, and then in her embarrassment she couldn't wait to get out of the car. So adult of her.

Tracy sighed and shook her head. Just as well. If they'd gotten together she had a feeling more than just his ribs would have been injured. Her heart would've taken the next hit.

A couple of bus stops later the woman lumbered off, and then it was her turn. Tracy navigated the busy aisle, leading with her briefcase so as not to knock anyone on her way past, and made her careful way down the steps into the congestion of early morning foot traffic.

The Medical Examiner's office was a block over and rather than fight the crowds, Tracy decided to cut through the mostly deserted park that separated the two streets. The path wove through a small copse of trees and meandered along a man-made brook where ducks and the odd swan swam, hoping for handouts from passersby.

Normally she enjoyed the restful scene and often spent lunch hours feeding the waterfowl but today it felt as though the shadows had eyes. Maybe she was still jittery from yesterday's encounter or maybe it was a sixth sense; either way her feet fairly flew across the expanse. She didn't draw a solid breath until she reached the front door of the office. Her heart was slow to settle back into place as she nodded her greetings to the security guard, receptionist, and some of the other lifers, as she liked to think of the longtime employees who liked to work the weekend, same as herself.

By the time the elevator whisked her up to the fourth floor and she made her way to the lab, Tracy was feeling almost normal. That is until she stepped into the room and met the serious gazes of Scott Anderson and her boss, Gil.

"Tracy. I believe you've met Mr. Anderson," Gil said as Scott stepped forward, hand outstretched.

So he was going to pretend she was merely an acquaintance, was he? Fine. Two could play that game.

She ignored his hand and strode around him to place her briefcase on her desk. "Sorry I'm late, my car was… indisposed. I had to grab the bus."

"You should have called," Scott said, and was echoed by Gil. The men glared at each other and Tracy's temper soared.

Men were Neanderthal idiots, every last one of them. And speaking of which…

"Where's Hank?" The man hadn't called in sick once in all the time they'd worked together.

Gil looked at Scot and then avoided her gaze, the two of them suddenly co-conspirators. Tracy's stomach dropped.

"What's going on?" She wrapped her fingers around the back of the chair in a death grip. A helpless ache tightened her throat until she could barely croak. "Tell me."

Scott took a step then halted when Gil moved around the desk first. He grasped her icy fingers in his, and met her gaze with saddened gray eyes.

"He's dead, honey. Home invasion."

When Scott first arrived this morning after calling, Gil Davis, Tracy's boss, had shown up to speak with him. He'd treated Scott with respect—not as the movie star—but as the lone survivor of a car accident, and he'd taken an immediate liking to the man.

"I'm sorry for your loss. If there's anything we can do…?" Gil asked and Scott shook his head. "I understand. Should you change your mind our doors are always open. Would you like to view the bodies now?"

Scott flinched. His stomach churned.

Now that the moment had arrived he was reluctant. Even though Lucas had paid him that extraordinary visit last night—then disappeared and left him thinking he was freaking crazy—the fact was both his friend and his sister's remains lay on cold metal slabs somewhere in this building.

"I think I'll wait for Dr. York if you don't mind."

"You know Tracy?" Gil asked, brushing a hand through his prematurely graying hair.

"We're… friends." Scott didn't know if she'd exactly agree with that assessment but they were more than mere acquaintances, especially after their kisses. The musky scent of her arousal and the sweet taste of her lips had embedded themselves in his memory.

"Good, she'll need her friends around her right now."

Scott frowned. Was he talking about the dog?

"You heard then?" he asked.

"Yeah, the police commissioner called me first thing this morning."

Not the dog then.

"What happened?" Scott demanded.

Gil looked at him askance. "I thought you knew. Tracy's partner, Hank, was murdered last night during a home invasion."

What the hell?

These attacks couldn't be random. Something was going on and Scott intended on finding out what before he lost someone else he cared for.

"What are you planning on doing about it?" Frustration and an unfamiliar helplessness rode him hard.

Gil frowned and crossed his arms over his chest, crumpling his Hermes tie in the process. "I don't know who you think you are, but we take care of our own around here."

"Yeah? That didn't work out so well for Tracy's partner, did it?" Scott slammed his hand down on the desk, rattling some loose pens. "You need to get her some security until this shit gets sorted out. Who do you think has a beef with this department?"

Gil turned away and rubbed a hand against the back of his neck. "I don't have a clue. The police are working on it, let's give them time to do their jobs."

Scott sank into a chair. Ever since the accident he'd felt like he was submerged under water and couldn't find his way to the top. The only positive thing in this new world he inhabited was seeing Lucas again—and meeting Tracy. He hated that she was in danger.

Lucas had tried to tell him last night he'd only returned to earth because Scott was in trouble, and it was his job to keep him safe.

Angered, Scott lashed out. "If you wanted to keep me safe maybe you shoulda watched where the fuck you were driving—buddy."

Lucas had paled. "Yeah man, you're right. And I'm more sorry than I can ever say. But, I think I've paid the price, don't you?"

He'd reached out then but Scott had jerked away, head down in misery. It was his stupid ass idea. All of it. Because of him his sister and his best friend were freakin' dead. Bile rose and he choked it down.

He'd turned, an apology on his lips, but Lucas had disappeared. Scott spent the rest of the night searching without hope. All he could do was pray he'd get another chance to make things right.

If Lucas ever showed himself again.

He'd needed to see his friend's remains and prove to himself this wasn't just a horrific dream, so he'd called first thing this morning.

And now here he was, watching his girl—even if she didn't think so—in the arms of another man.

Scott stood back, fists clenched, while Tracy crumpled into her boss's arms. He ached to be the one holding her, offering comfort and anything else she might need.

The coincidences were piling up and he didn't like it.

Chapter 13

Lucas grunted, landing flat on his back on the beach near the same cabin where he'd first met the Lord. The stars, large enough to touch, twinkled merrily in the sky mocking his discomfort. Storm clouds in rich shades of purple, pink, and navy blue hovered on the far side of the lake. Seemed kinda weird, considering where he was and all. So much for heaven being butterflies and daffodils.

His side burned like he had a bad case of road-rash. He lifted his shirt for a look and grimaced at the angry-looking red welt running along his washboard abs. It was festering. He needed to find shelter and some medical aid.

He climbed gingerly to his feet and had a look around. The campfire they'd enjoyed the fish at the other night had burned itself out and was nothing more than a blackened mess, rather like his life. Shivering as a blast of frigid air hit his skin, Lucas headed for the cabin.

He stumbled up the rough-hewn stairs. noting the old-fashioned rocking chairs on the porch facing the lake. A nice spot to relax on a warm summer's evening if you weren't an angel tasked with saving human lives.

His fist made a dull thud against the solid pine door. When no one answered he tried the knob and found it turned smoothly beneath his hand. He entered slowly, but the large room with an open beam ceiling was empty.

Making his way over to a single oversized porcelain farm sink, he turned on the taps. A stack of snowy white towels sat conveniently on the counter to the right but he hesitated, loath to ruin them. There wasn't much choice though, he needed to get the wound cleaned.

Lucas dropped a hand towel in the scalding water then stripped out of his soiled shirt. After sluicing his face and neck he wrung out the towel and eased it against his side. Sweat broke out over his back and forearms, the pain almost unbearable, but he forced himself to repeat the procedure two more times before he was satisfied he'd done all that he could.

Weak-kneed, he searched for a place to sit and found an oversized tweed and leather sofa in front of a blackened stone fireplace taking up almost an entire wall. There was kindling already piled in the hearth and a match on the mantle so he took that as an invitation and lit the fire before lowering himself gingerly onto the couch. A beer and a hockey game and he'd be set. He leaned back and closed his eyes, figuring on a couple minutes of rest.

When he awoke he was lying stretched out on the sofa and a soft wool blanket had been thrown over his body. He swung his legs down and sat up, wincing at the tug on his side.

A female hummed quietly by the sink, her slender back almost hidden by a waterfall of golden brown tresses. The tips brushed the top of a skintight pair of well-worn jeans that lovingly cupped a heart-shaped ass. She seemed oblivious to the fact Lucas was awake, and continued her chore of cutting and arranging a giant bouquet of meadow flowers into a crystal vase. She made a pretty picture framed by the gingham curtains lining the plate-glass window. He cleared his throat to get her attention, curious about who she might be and what she was doing there.

Startled, she dropped the knife and it clanged into the sink. Her head drooped like one of her flowers. Then she swung around, her arms crossed defensively.

Lucas froze, shocked to his core. What kind of sick joke was this?

"Natalya?" he croaked.

Tracy sobbed until she couldn't cry any more. Her chest was nothing more than a giant aching hole. Hank was dead. There would be no more stupid morgue jokes. No newspaper funnies left on her desk. No more bags of her favorite sugary donuts at coffee break.

No Hank.

They'd been friends and partners for most of the five years she'd worked here. What was she going to do without him?

Gil passed her a tissue and she blotted the worst of her tears away before meeting his concerned gaze.

"You going to be all right?"

She nodded, there wasn't much choice. "Do they have any suspects?"

Gil looked away. "Not yet."

Great.

None of this made any sense. What was the common denominator? Her eyes widened as she swung around to face Scott seated in front of her desk.

"This is all your fault." She leaned over and slammed her hands on the desk. "Everything that's happened started after your friend and sister arrived here. What kind of crap were you guys into before that accident?"

He didn't answer.

"Tell me," she cried, her fingers tingling with the urge to shake him until he admitted his guilt.

"Tracy," Gil warned.

Scott shook his head and latched onto her hands, refusing to let go when she would have pulled away.

"I can see where that beautiful head of yours is going, but you're wrong. Lucas and I have never gotten into the drug scene. Ever," he emphasized. "I'm not going to lie to you, there were plenty of parties and more than enough chances to try the shit out, but we weren't into it, okay?"

He squeezed her hands, then let go before standing. "I'm not sure what this is about, but we're going to find out. I have money; I can hire private investigators to do some digging around. There has to be a link somewhere."

"We don't…"

"No thank you," Gil spoke over top Tracy. "We don't need anyone coming in and muddying the waters. The Chicago P.D. know what they're doing, let them do their jobs."

Gil strode to the door, stopping with his hand on the knob. "Don't go anywhere, Anderson. They'll probably want to question you soon." He turned to Tracy. "If you need some time, I understand. Take a break, it'll help." Then he nodded and walked out, closing the door behind him.

An awkward silence fell over the room. Now that she had calmed down, Tracy was embarrassed by her outburst. It wasn't like her to be so emotional. But then, she'd never had a partner get murdered before either.

"Do you honestly believe I have something to do with this?" Scott moved around the desk until he stood directly in front of her. He tipped her chin up.

She met his gaze defiantly. "I don't know, do I? We barely know each other."

Instead of getting mad like she expected, his lips quirked. His thumb brushed slowly along her bottom lip and her eyes slid to half-mast. She gulped, unable to deny the sensual reaction to his touch.

"Don't," she whispered.

His mouth took over where his thumb left off, feathering gently along the edge of her lips until she opened on a sigh. "Don't what?"

Their lips clung, bound by invisible threads.

"Deny that we have something between us?" he asked.

More teasing, exploring kisses meant to drive her out of her freaking mind.

"I'm not," he murmured, answering himself. He stepped in closer, so close she could feel the exaggerated beat of his heart and the heat radiating from his big body. The all too evident ridge of his arousal.

Even as she met him kiss for kiss a small voice in her head kept asking if she knew what she was doing, who she was kissing.

The answer; not a freaking clue.

But she meant to find out.

Chapter 14

Lucas scrubbed his eyes and took a deep, steadying breath before he chanced another glance at the woman he'd just been ogling. Nothing had changed. Natalya stood before him in a shirt that was too damn short—was that a diamond winking at him from her belly button?—and a pair of jeans that looked as though they were painted onto her lithe frame.

Shit. Natalya's here.

Which meant she must also be in transition?

Cursing their luck wouldn't change a thing, even if it would be a good momentary release. It was his fucking fault this was happening and now others were paying the price.

"Aren't you happy to see me?" she asked, looking impossibly young and innocent. The sunlight streamed through the window behind her, bathing her body in a warm, ethereal glow.

Lucas rose, moved to her side, and held out his arms. "C'mere. Of course I'm glad to see you."

She flowed into his arms and laid her head against his chest.

"I just wish it wasn't here," he whispered into her hair, inhaling the fresh scent of the meadow on her skin. He'd spent so many years thinking of her as Scott's little sister, it was hard reconciling the undeniable attraction coursing through his veins. He'd never realized how petite she was. The top of her head barely brushed his chin, and his arms wrapped around her narrow back, came conveniently close to the sides of her breasts.

Feeling like a pervert, he kissed her forehead and set her back to get a better look at her familiar, yet somehow different, features. He didn't remember those cheekbones being quite so high. Nor had he noticed the lush fullness of her mouth. Jerking his gaze from her lips, Lucas relaxed a little when he met her blue-green eyes. The mischievous smile lighting their depths was one he knew well.

"Well, this is a fine pickle I've gotten us into," he muttered.

Nat giggled, the sound a sparkling brook that quenched his tortured soul. From the time she was little, he and Scott had known she was special. Different from the rest of the hard-scrabble kids trying to eke out their place in a world that refused to cut them a break. Her bubbly personality and enjoyment with the simplest of pleasures—whether it was a tulip poking out of the hard ground, the lazy buzzing of a bee, or the gift of a cookie he'd filched from the local supermarket—made his life bearable during those tough times.

"At least we have each other," she said. She leaned to the right, her gaze searching the room behind him. "Where's Scott?"

She doesn't know.

It was one thing for her to go off to college and not see her family until the holidays, but this…

She and Scott had always been close. All three of them were. She was going to take this hard.

"Natalya…" He grabbed her hands and waited until she met his somber gaze. "He made it, honey. We're all alone."

The excitement shining in her expression slowly died, leaving behind bewilderment and pain. "How? What happened, Lucas? Where are we exactly?" Moisture formed at the corners of her eyes and she dashed it away. "The last thing I remember is that van coming right for us and Scott pushing my head down, then… nothing until I woke up here."

So she'd probably been in the cabin while he'd been receiving his new duties. The Big Guy had to know how he'd feel about seeing her. Why keep it a secret? And why let him in on it now?

She stared at him with so much trust and affection. Cursing himself for the asshole he was, Lucas sidestepped her questions. "Do you want to know how Scott is doing? I've seen him since—you know—this."

The clouds in her eyes dispersed, leaving elation in its wake. "Of course I do. Is he okay then? Does he miss us? When can I see him?"

The last was said in a plea that ripped at his heart.

He turned and strode across the room to the fireplace, adding another log and stirring the embers, anything so he wouldn't have to see her disappointment. The truth was, unless the boss gave the all clear, she might never get to see her brother again.

"Lucas?"

He jumped. She'd followed him and now crouched in front of the fresh sparks, her hands held out for warmth.

"I'm not going to, am I?" she asked, her attention on the quickly spiraling flames.

Lucas gazed at the silken fall of honey-gold hair hiding her expression and cursed the God that would do this to someone so undeserving.

"I don't know, honey. I just don't know."

Scott was slow to pull out of the sensual haze a few kisses from Tracy induced. The effect was like a bomb on his heart, the blood pounding so hard in his ears he'd barely heard the phone she turned to answer. Their chemistry was off the charts crazy, yet he had no idea where he stood with her. It was maddening. And exciting. She was different from his usual hook-ups—not that he classed her anywhere near the same category as them—and he liked her. A lot.

She pulled a file closer, met his gaze, then returned to her call. He could still see the remnants of tears on her cheeks and ached to kiss them away. He knew something of how she must be feeling, having just lost Lucas and Natalya himself. There were no words that could give comfort in a situation like theirs, but having her in his life the past couple of days made a big difference. Hard to imagine that's all it was; two days. Their connection was instantaneous from the moment he saw her crouched over that poor dog. If he were a person who believed in fate, he'd have to say they were meant to meet.

Tracy murmured goodbye to whoever was on the other end of the line, then sighed and sank into her chair. Elbows on the cherry wood desktop, she combed her hands through the chestnut waves of her hair. "We can't do that any more."

"Do what?" he asked, knowing full well what she meant.

She waved a vague hand between them. "You know what I mean." Letting it fall to her lap, she stared at him with haunted green eyes. "You confuse me. And no, don't you smile."

He wiped the smirk away.

"I like my life structured and organized, but ever since you came into the picture it's been anything but ordinary. You're messing with my Zen, Anderson."

Scott's lips quirked. He couldn't help it. She looked like a little kid who just found out the Easter bunny had given up his day job.

"I don't mean to mess with your Zen, as you put it." Poor baby, she did look frazzled, and a little scared.

He leaned forward and held his hand palm up on the desk. "I'm sorry you lost your partner. Why don't you let me take you away from here for the day?" She gave her head an undecided shake.

"C'mon, Trace. You heard your boss. He encouraged you to take some time off."

"What about you? Aren't you here to see your sister and friend?"

Scott looked down. "It can wait. I'd rather remember them as they were."

Her hand gently entwined with his fingers. He lifted his gaze and got lost in her eyes. They reminded him of a meadow he'd seen on a shoot in Ireland. He could cheerfully spend the rest of his days waking up to that view.

Holy shit.

He was in love. How the hell did that happen?

He'd played parts before that included love at first sight and always thought the screenwriters needed to jump on the reality train more often. Who believed in that crap anyway? But it had always paid the bills and gained him fans, so he'd gone along for the ride.

But this. It made no sense, and yet all the sense in the world.

"So, what do you say? Want to run away with me?"

Tracy scowled. "Be serious," she said.

He squeezed her fingers and met her defiant gaze. "Oh, I am, sweetheart. I am."

It looked as though his work was going to be cut out for him. "C'mon, it'll be fun. We can go for a picnic in the park. I don't know about you, but I haven't had a good meal for a while. I'm starved."

She looked him up and down and his heart kicked up a fuss. Suddenly, food wasn't the only thing he was hungry for.

"I guess, but we can't go far. I want to stick around in case Gil hears something about Hank. And I need to pick up Sugar-Bear today." She pushed her chair back and stood, nervously smoothing her skirt down that delectable ass.

"Sugar-Bear?" He shook his head. Poor mutt was going to get a complex.

Tracy gave him the stink-eye. "What's wrong with it? He's as big as a bear and he's a sweetheart. It seemed rather obvious."

He held up a hand in peace, and then completely ruined it by laughing. Yep, she was one in a million all right.

Chapter 15

T racy stole sideways glances at the handsome profile of her date as he negotiated the heavy Chicago traffic. A date. She couldn't remember the last time she'd done something so spontaneous. There were any number of open cases on her desk she should be working on, including Hank's, but for the moment nothing else mattered except spending a little more time with this man. He affected her more than she cared to admit.

He had led her outside the ME's office to the convertible Mustang parked in the visitor lot and handed her onto the sleek leather passenger seat. Shell-shocked after their kiss, she hadn't said anything when he lowered the top, started the engine with its deep-throated growl, and pulled away from the lot.

Curiosity had kicked in now, though.

"Where are we going?"

"Grant Park," he said, shooting her a quick glance as he signaled onto Congress Parkway. The wind flirted with his sandy blond hair and blew a lock over his forehead. With his leather jacket and sky-blue eyes, it was no wonder thousands of women swooned at his movies. He had the whole *James Dean* vibe going—it was difficult to resist.

Soon they were driving into the park. Scott found a space and pulled in, shifting the gearshift into first with his left hand in an economy of motion, then yanking up on the handbrake before he shut the engine down.

The sudden silence made her nervous. She tucked a strand of hair behind her ear and cleared her throat. "This is nice."

Brilliant observation, Watson.

"Yeah, it is." He gave a melancholy smile. "We came here to show my sister the sights the day of the crash."

Oh, Scott.

She touched his casted arm in sympathy. "We don't have to stay."

He stared out the window, then pulled his keys and met her gaze. "I want to share this with you."

Her heart squeezed. She swallowed back the tears and forced a teasing grin. "Okay then, hotshot. What's for lunch? I'm starving."

Scott slanted her a grateful look and opened his door. "I stopped at a diner on my way to your office this morning and had them do us up a basket—on the off-chance you'd actually agree to go out with me."

His backward grin was engaging, and she hopped out to join him at the rear of the car, her emotions as effervescent as the bottle of champagne he added to the basket.

He lifted the hamper and a red and white checked blanket from the trunk, slammed the lid, and held out well-tanned fingers dangling below the white cast. "Shall we?"

Tracy hesitated, then accepted his hand, luxuriating in the hard warmth of his touch. They began their walk across the lot and entered the park proper, stopping to watch a wedding shoot at the iconic Bellingham Fountain. Grant Park nestled on the shores of Lake Michigan, a favorite with the locals. Tracy envied the obvious adoration of the groom for his beautiful bride. Sometimes she wondered if her choice of career stopped men from looking at her in a romantic light. Or maybe it was just her. Not that she was a hag—or at least she hoped not—but she wasn't someone men generally stopped and stared at, either. *Victoria's Secret* wasn't going to be calling her for a contract any time soon.

And where had all this sudden self-condemnation come from? She was normally a fairly confident person. Just because every woman they passed took second and third looks at her companion... It didn't bother her. Much.

She stopped to admire a gorgeously laid out flowerbed filled with bright red tulips, nasturtiums, and daisies. Scott chose a nearby knoll, and set the hamper down before fighting one-handed with the blanket.

Tracy hurried over and grabbed an end, laying it out on the lush green grass.

"Well, that's good to know," she said, sinking down and kicking off her heels to bury her toes in the grass.

Scott towered above her, his body casting a shadowy outline over her legs. He grinned and crouched down with only a slight grimace this time. "What's good to know?"

She brushed away a nosy fly before answering. "Just that you're human like the rest of us mere mortals, that's all."

He huffed out a laugh and sank onto his butt, long jean-clad legs stretched out in front of him. He wore tan cowboy boots with intricate stitching. It was much too easy to picture him on the side of her bed, without a shirt to hide the taut muscles of his back, as he worked to pull those boots off.

Whew, that sun was warm today.

"Of course I'm human," he answered. "And if you keep looking at me like that, you're going to find out how much." The heated intent in his eyes made it clear that they were traveling the same wavelength.

Oh, boy.

Embarrassed, Tracy turned to the hamper and opened the lid, but Scott's hand on her arm made her stop and raise her gaze to his.

"Why do you do that?" he asked, brushing a curl behind her ear.

She shivered in response, then shrugged to cover it up. "Do what?"

"Turn away every time I tell you how much you turn me on. It's natural, you know." He sat back. "We're two healthy adults who happen to find each other attractive. I say we should explore the possibilities."

Well, of course he did. What red-blooded American male was going to say no when a woman practically threw herself at his feet?

Her lips twisted into a dry smile. "Why don't we just enjoy the afternoon and take it from there?"

He leaned back on his good elbow and crossed his ankles, which did interesting things to the fit of his jeans—not that she was looking or anything.

"Okay, Doc. Whatever you say."

Scott worked to keep his expression casual, but holy hell, the woman was testing his integrity. He didn't think she realized just what those eat-me-up eyes did to his equilibrium. He was the one supposed to be seducing her, not the other way around.

And the kicker was, she didn't know she was doing it.

If they weren't sitting in the middle of a public park, he wouldn't have been able to control the urge to tumble her right there. As it was, he was going to be walking with a limp if he didn't cool things down soon.

"Hand me the wine and I'll crack the bottle," he suggested.

She looked at him doubtfully, but handed it over nonetheless. He placed the bottle in the crook of his arm, just above the cast, and gave a sharp twist with his hand. The top popped and bubbly exploded, causing Tracy to jump and laugh. He watched, fascinated. Her eyes sparkled when she thought something was humorous. And she had this thing where she'd suck her bottom lip into her mouth and crush it between her teeth. It was so sexy he had to glance away before he was the one embarrassed.

He held the wine up and waited for her to find glasses, then poured them each a healthy shot.

"You trying to get me drunk, Anderson?" she teased, taking an appreciative sip. Her tongue peeked out to lick up the excess.

He groaned, he couldn't help it.

"Are you okay?" she asked, concern turning her eyes mossy.

How to answer that.

Sure, but I'd be better if you came and climbed onto my lap.

Yeah, that's probably not going to work. Damn.

"Just a spasm, no worries. Why don't you see what they packed for us?"

She gazed at him skeptically, then twisted to remove the contents of the basket. The swell of her breasts pressed against the material of her shirt and his heartbeat swelled into a crescendo.

He could see a long cold shower on his horizon.

"There's chicken, prawns, cheese, crackers—oh, oh perfect." She pulled a giant slice of German chocolate cake out in a plastic domed container. "Let's start with this."

Scott laughed, absurdly happy he'd pleased her. Already the lines of stress from this morning were easing and she was looking more relaxed. The dull noise of traffic was accompanied by the nearby sound of singing birds and the odd curious insect. It all worked to create a little bubble of contentment, one he hated to break.

He took a sip of his wine and watched in amusement as she dived into the cake with the exuberance of a child. She looked at him and placed a portion on her fork, hovering it in the general area of his face.

"Try this, Anderson. It's amazing." She leaned closer to give him a taste and lost her balance. The cake slid to the blanket and she landed right where he wanted her, against his chest.

"Oomph. I'm so sorry," she exclaimed, her eyes huge and filled with amusement.

"I'm not," he whispered, right before he got his own taste of amazing.

Chapter 16

Lucas stared down at the bright blonde head by his side and cursed his helplessness. It had always been his personal goal to make sure Natalya had whatever she needed. He couldn't explain to himself why it mattered so much, just that it did. Which made this situation all the worse. He needed to find a way for her to connect with her brother so that she could see for herself that he was okay. But how? It wasn't like there was an elevator down to ground level or anything. He didn't even know how he'd gotten there himself. It just sorta—happened.

And then there was the issue of his new partner, Mike. He hadn't seen the other man since he left him at his house, but could guess what he was going through. Losing your whole family like that... it sucked.

Lucas had gone over his own accident a hundred times already. If only he hadn't turned his head and been distracted just then.

If wishes were horses...

"Have you talked to anyone else since you arrived?" he asked Nat, curious as to who might be hanging in limbo around here.

"No, you're the first." She stabbed at a log, causing a shower of sparks, before she rose and placed the poker in an ornate stand on the hearth. She turned to face him and the gratitude shining in her expression set him back a step.

"Do you realize how happy I am that you're here? I was so scared. I thought I was going to be alone forever." Her eyes welled up, becoming deep pools he could cheerfully drown in.

"Nat," he said, and held open his arms, helpless against her pain.

She hesitated for a nano-second, then heaved a giant sigh of relief and snuggled in tight to his chest. Her arms crept around his back and Lucas was going to hell for sure, it felt so good. His cheek rubbed against her silky hair and he closed his eyes, the better to let his other senses soak up the scent of sunshine and summer meadows.

When she glanced up, it was the most natural thing in the world to lean down and touch his lips to the smile on hers.

The room tilted.

Lucas pulled away, cursing under his breath, but Natalya murmured a protest and lifted her hands to jam them in his hair, tugging him closer. Her mouth flirted shyly with his, leaving soft butterfly kisses that drove him Over. The. Edge.

And then there was no turning back.

He groaned and slanted his mouth over hers, taking control and showing her this was no game they played. His thumb caressed the side of her face, reveling in the soft texture of her creamy skin. Up close she was even more enticing, and he was going down for the count.

She stood on her toes for leverage and the fullness of her breasts strained against his chest, the hard nubs turning him inside out. He'd waited a lifetime for this moment.

"Do you know what you're doing to me?" His voice was little more than a growl, filled with the effort of holding his passion under lockdown. If Scott knew...

He grabbed her arms and held her away. "Stop, Nat. We can't do this."

She looked as dazed as he felt. It was all Lucas could do to step away from the sweet temptation of flushed cheeks and bee-stung lips.

"Don't look at me like that. You know this is wrong." He smacked the fireplace mantle. "Dammit, you're too young. Barely more than a teenager, for crying out loud."

Natalya snorted, and swung away, striding over to the sink and running a glass of water. She took a long drink, set the glass on the counter, then turned and leaned against the ledge with her arms crossed and cheeks flushed.

"You done?" she asked.

Why did he suddenly feel like a kid about to get a talking to?

"Listen, Nat..."

She straightened and poked a finger in his direction. "No, you listen. I've followed after you like a besotted idiot for as long as I can remember. I watched you take out girl after girl and hated every single one of them. But, it was okay, you know," Tears leaked from the corners of her eyes and she brushed them away impatiently, "because they never stuck. And as long as you were dating different women, you weren't falling in love. Which meant maybe… maybe I had a chance."

She moved closer. "Lucas, we aren't kids anymore. You don't have to protect me." Her hands rested on his bare chest, right over the pounding of his heart. "Why do you think I came to Chicago?"

He stiffened, somehow knowing he wasn't going to like what she had to say.

"I thought you wanted to see how the other half lived?" He was hoping to lighten the mood, but she only gave him a sad quirk of the lips.

"I've met someone," she said, and his heart literally stopped. She hesitated as though waiting for his blessing, or some fucking thing. When he stayed silent, she sighed.

"I *came*," she added forcefully, "to see if we'd ever stand a chance, or if this was going to be goodbye."

Lucas stared down into her precious face and didn't know what to say. It was only just recently that he even admitted he had those kinds of feelings for his best friend's sister. Never mind the freaking L word, which she seemed to be looking to hear from him. What a mess.

"Nat…"

She pulled away, as though sensing what he was going to say.

Loud clapping from the doorway made them both jump as though a bomb had gone off.

Mike stood there like a black cloud, his face a grim mask. "Well, isn't this sweet? Where's the chocolate and roses?"

"Shut up, man. You don't know nothing about this," Lucas growled. "Where the hell have you been?"

Mike slammed the door shut and clomped over to make his ornery self right at home on the couch.

Natalya turned white and swayed alarmingly.

Lucas grabbed her arm and led her to the other chair. He brushed her forehead and found it clammy. "What's wrong? You look like you've seen a ghost."

She stared at Mike like he was an anomaly, which he was, but hey.

"He's... he's the man in the van," she whispered. "The one you hit in the accident."

The words smashed Lucas in the solar plexus with the force of a gunshot. He froze, shocked. Surely, God wouldn't place him with the one man who had every right to hate his guts?

Natalya's scream was the only warning he had before two hundred pounds of enraged angel flew at him, knocking him off his heels.

He rolled to the side, taking Mike with him in an effort to protect Nat. The blows came hard and fast, slam after slam hitting his ears, nose, and mouth, but Lucas did nothing to defend himself. In some screwed up part of his brain the pain was cathartic.

What hurt more were the animal sounds of agony coming from the other man's tortured soul.

A vicious jab to the nose sent blood spraying, hitting their faces and the fluffy white rug beneath them. Natalya yelled something—his ears were ringing so he couldn't make it out—and rushed into the fray, pushing and shoving to get Mike to move. Lucas tried to tell her to get back, but the words wouldn't form. Mike reared up, threw out an arm, and sent her tumbling against the fireplace.

She fell backward and tripped, going down hard. Her head hit the hearth with a bone-jarring crack and then there was only silence.

Chapter 17

Lucas shoved Mike away, and crawled across to Natalya's prone body. She lay crumpled on the floor. Cast-off like a broken doll. He gently brushed the golden strands of hair back with shaking fingers. Delicate blue veins covered her eyelids and half-moon lashes lay thick upon her pale cheeks. He carefully lifted her close to his aching chest.

"It was an accident," Mike croaked.

"Grab me a cool cloth." How was he supposed to get her any help up here? What was the sense of being dead if a person could still get hurt?

"Any idea how to get hold of the Big Guy?" he growled when Mike handed a couple moist towels over.

"You mean besides the obvious?" Mike held up steepled fingers. "If that doesn't work, I have no clue."

For real?

Lucas had given up praying way back in middle grade when his grandpa died, and his mom re-married the drunk from down the street. It never seemed as though anyone was listening then, so he didn't hold out much hope for now.

"Have you seen anyone else around this dump?" Never mind that the cabin was nicer than most of the homes he'd lived in.

Mike shook his head and moved to the window.

Lucas' gaze dropped to Nat. If anything she seemed paler, damn near as white as the towel on her forehead.

He didn't look up when the door opened and closed, just continued to watch over the girl in his arms. No, not a girl. Natalya had become a woman. A woman he couldn't lose. He swore to do whatever it took to bring her back.

Even praying to a Lord who'd never heard him cry.

Tracy watched *as lips* that had fueled thousands of female fantasies edged nearer and wondered if she was going to hyperventilate. Scott Anderson was about to kiss her. How had this happened? And even more, how was she going to go back to her normal, everyday life after he left?

Then his mouth touched hers and everything went into slow-mo. Every inch of skin became incredibly sensitized, even the follicles of her hair. It was crazy. And wildly exhilarating. He smelled of wine and chocolate and she was never going to get over him.

His hands delved into her hair, holding her head in place for his kisses. There was a reason he was a movie sex symbol. The man knew how to kiss. Her toes curled. The heat radiating from his big frame acted like an aphrodisiac, lulling her mind and rejuvenating her body.

This day was going to go down as one of the best days of her life. And even the guilt over feeling this way while her partner lay dead, couldn't darken her mood. Hank would've been the first to tell her to enjoy this time, and she intended to do just that, before life came crashing back down.

The laughter of people nearby broke through the sensual haze.

Scott dropped his head back on the blanket and stared up at the sky, his breathing strained. Tracy lowered her cheek to his chest and reveled in his increased heart rate, proof that he too was affected by their lovemaking.

"Whoever suggested a public park should be shot," he grumbled.

A husky laugh escaped. That was one of the things she liked most about him, his sense of humor was contagious.

She sat up and wrapped her arms around bent knees. "I think this was a good idea actually. Most definitely safer."

It took most of their lunch together to get her pulse halfway back to a normal range. Afterward, they took a short walk and admired some of the beautiful sculptures dotting the area. When they returned to the blanket they succumbed to the afternoon sunshine and took a nap.

Tracy awoke a short time later and snuck furtive glances at the man snoozing by her side. She wished they could remain here forever. Their teasing kisses earlier had filled her with the hot urge to give in to him, take what he offered. The question was whether she could have an affair with him without getting hurt.

"I can hear you thinking from here," Scott murmured. He turned his head and gazed at her with slumberous eyes as blue as the sky above their heads. He really was the handsomest man alive.

She smiled and started to pack up their stuff. "We better go soon. I need to go get Sugar-Bear before the clinic closes."

Scott grabbed her wrist, stalling her movements. "Is that all? Something's bothering you. Talk to me, Trace."

She looked at their joined hands and fought the lump growing in her throat.

"You and I won't work, Scott." She bravely met his gaze, determined to make him understand.

He sat up, all lean muscle and fluid movements, reminding her of a big cat. He brought her hand to his lips for a light kiss, then let it go and rose to his feet, stretching languidly before reaching for the hamper.

"We better go if we want to beat traffic. The clinic's across town, right?"

Tracy nodded, bemused. "That's it? No argument?"

He looked back and grinned. "I learned a long time ago it never pays to argue with a woman." He swung the hamper in the direction of the parked cars, "You ready?"

Perversely, now she wanted to stay put. If they left this little retreat they'd created, it would become part of the past, something she'd look back on and wonder why she hadn't taken a chance.

Picking up the blanket, Tracy followed.

Once they were in the car and driving, she turned in her seat, curiosity getting the best of her. "Tell me about Lucas and Natalya."

Scott gave her a startled glance before refocusing on the busy roadways. "What do you want to know?"

At least he hadn't shut her down, it was a start.

She looked out the window at the sparkling blue of Lake Michigan and shrugged. "All of it. Where did you grow up? How did you meet?" She met his darkening gaze and knew he was going to make light of his answer. She shook her head. "Don't. I really want to know. They were important to you. It matters to me, okay?"

He hesitated, then dipped his chin in a short, sharp nod, fingers turning white on the steering wheel.

Tracy frowned. It wasn't her intent to upset him. She had a genuine interest in his background, but if it was going to hurt...

"We come from an area of town people who have money go to when they want to ease their conscience with some charity work." He shot her a look brimming with old resentments. "You get what I'm sayin'? We had nothing, less than nothing, really." He gave the car a shot of gas and jumped lanes. "Except our dreams. They couldn't take those away."

"Scott." Tracy's heart ached for the boy still hidden within the body of the man-who-had-everything sitting beside her. "Forget it. I didn't mean to bring up bad memories."

He laughed, but it was little more than a harsh cough.

"You don't get it," he said. "The memories are what kept us going. They fueled our fire to succeed." He looked at her and his smile was bittersweet. "And we did. We made it. Too bad Lucas and my sister aren't here to enjoy it, right?"

Tracy gulped around the fist wedged in her throat and forced an answering smile. "They're still around, Scott. Just because you can't see them, doesn't mean they're gone." She placed a hand over his heart. "They're here, right here. You have to believe that."

He leaned over and gave her a quick peck on the mouth, but didn't answer. And though they sat side by side, she'd never felt more alone.

Chapter 18

By the time they went through the adoption process and received instructions on Sugar-Bear's care, it was late afternoon. The dog was quiet, but his big brown eyes seemed to say he was happy to be going home. The stark white bandages looked incongruous against the white and black patches of his fur.

Tracy laid the blanket they'd used for the picnic across the backseat and Sugar-Bear climbed in on his own, though he moved rather stiffly. He turned a couple of circles then laid down with his head on the middle console.

"I think you've made another conquest," Scott teased.

If only.

She got in carefully so as not to bump the dog's nose, and patted his head. She wasn't sure about owning a pet, but there was no way she could let him go to the pound either. They'd been through too much together. At least she had a fenced in backyard attached to her condo. He'd have a place to run and do his thing. It would be nice to have company, and the added security. She'd make it work.

"They like their ears rubbed," Scott said, and showed her the technique. Sugar-Bear groaned his agreement. "Are you really going to stick with that name? I saw you write it on the adoption papers." His gaze was warm with humor.

Never one to go down without a fight, she turned to the dog. "Why not? I think it suits him. He seems like a sweetheart."

Scott started the car. "Yeah, but that doesn't mean he wants a prissy tag." He turned out of the lot. "Where to?"

"Just take me home, if you don't mind. I can go to the pet store from there." She'd already taken up far too much of his time. There must be an endless list of activities in an actor's life.

To prove her point, Scott's phone chose that moment to ring. He sent her a quick glance, then hit the car's answer button.

"Where the hell are you? I've been trying to reach you all day. Do you even care about the mess you've left me in?"

Sugar-Bear didn't care for the attitude-ridden voice coming in over the speakers. He growled low in his throat and sat up, his ears laid back.

Tracy shushed the animal and looked at Scott's expressionless face.

"What do you want, Ray?" They came to a stop light. His fingers tapped the wheel impatiently.

"Don't give me that shit. Last I knew you were lying in a goddamn hospital bed. And while I'm cleaning up from that disaster, you go and walk out? What the hell, man?"

Scott stiffened. "Disaster? Frickin' right, it's a disaster. I lost my family, you asshole."

Tracy touched his tensed arm. He met her worried gaze and sighed.

"Look, Ray, I need some time. I'm sorry to leave you holding the bag, but then that's what we pay you the big bucks for, right?" His voice lifted with forced humor.

There was a tense silence, then Ray laughed. "Yeah, sure. Okay, give me a call when you're ready to come back. And Scott... don't let it be too long."

Click, the line went dead.

The light turned green and the Mustang's tires squealed, sending Tracy back in her seat.

"So... that was awkward," she muttered.

A choked laugh eased the grim line of Scott's mouth. "Sorry about that. My agent tends to forget who works for whom."

She looked at him curiously. "Have you been together long?"

Scott glanced at the upscale stereo system. She frowned when he used his casted arm to turn the thing on and search until he found a jazz station to listen to.

"You could ask for help, you know."

He shook his head. "Nah. We're... I mean, I'm used to handling things on my own." A dark shadow passed over his face. "Ray was the first one to take us seriously when we hit L.A., mind you we looked pretty rough back then." He shot her a devilish grin. "Two teenage boys let loose in the City of Angels. Trouble with a capital T, right?"

Oh, yeah. Tracy could well imagine the wild parties those two probably found. No doubt it was a real eye-opening experience, whether they came from a bad background or not. Los Angeles wasn't exactly known for its kinder, gentler side.

"He took you under his wing and taught you the ropes then?" She was fascinated by this insight into his past.

"Something like that, yeah," Scott said and signaled into the pet store lot.

"You didn't need to do this, you know." She frowned as he pulled into a space near the back alley, and looked back to check on Sugar-Bear. He'd settled down and gone to sleep, his nose tucked under his front paw. He reminded her of The Joker in the Batman movies. One leg was white, while the other was half black. The rest of his coat looked like someone threw a gallon of paint. He was a mismatch, just like her.

Scott shut off the car and met her gaze. "Maybe I'm not ready to say goodbye just yet."

A warm rush of emotion filled her chest. "I'm glad."

He leaned over and brushed her lips with his, and a shiver of awareness shot down her spine.

"You shouldn't look so surprised," he murmured. "You feel it too, I can tell. There's something between us, doc, and I plan on finding out what."

Was he suggesting he cared? Because that's what it sounded like to her. Did they really stand a chance? It was hard to comprehend; the medical examiner and the movie star—see your local film guide. Just the logistics of it baffled her mind. But, maybe she was jumping the gun. He hadn't actually said he planned to stick around long term. She feared he had the capability to hurt her. Tracy wasn't sure she wanted to take the risk.

"We better get in there," she said, backing away literally and figuratively. "They'll be closing soon."

Scott hesitated, his eyes a stormy blue-grey, then he took a deep breath and opened the car door. "Yeah sure, let's go."

Tracy opened her door and slid the seat forward for Sugar-Bear, all the while feeling as though she'd just lost something priceless.

It took them a good hour or more to wander the big department store. Who knew there were so many kinds of dog food? Not to mention, treats, toys, shampoos, beds. It was dizzying for someone who'd never had a pet before. Sugar-Bear was the perfect gentleman, showing only a mild interest in any of the other canines they came across. Tracy hadn't been sure what to expect. Maybe this owning a dog thing wouldn't be so bad.

When they finally got up to the till, Scott insisted on buying, and though it went against the grain, Tracy let him. He looked as though pride was about the only thing holding him upright. His ribs must be killing him after all that walking, though he never complained.

"Sugar-Bear thanks you for his new bed," she joked as they left the store. It had turned dark while they were inside and the fall air had a definite bite. She pulled her sweater closed and tightened her grip on the dog leash.

"I'm surprised you didn't go for the pink one, it would suit the name," he teased back. He pushed the filled cart one-handed down the sidewalk. "We really need to rethink that, for his sake. How about Duke?"

Tracy laughed. "My dog is secure in his masculinity. He doesn't need a macho name to prove it." She glanced down and grinned at Sugar-Bear prancing down the walk.

The shopping cart clattered as Scott started across the pitted lot to the car. She could see he was struggling with it, but knew he'd turn her offer of help away.

Men, always with the stubborn.

A set of lights pierced the darkness. Tracy squinted to see as the vehicle picked up speed. Sugar-Bear growled and pulled up short. The car seemed to steer right for them. Scott shouted a warning and grabbed her hand, tugging her out of the way seconds before the bumper slammed into the cart and sent it flying with a horrible screeching of metal on metal.

They fell to the ground in a tangle of arms and legs, Sugar-Bear barking uncontrollably. She lay gasping for breath, shocked by their close call. Couldn't the idiot see them? Admittedly the parking lot could use better lighting, but still, there was no way whoever it was should have missed seeing the gleam from the cart at least.

Sugar-Bear whined and licked her chin. Tracy reassured him she was okay, then brushed him away and turned to look at Scott. He'd sat up and was staring after the disappearing car's taillights.

His gaze was grim when he met hers. "You okay?"

She nodded, and buried her trembling fingers into the dog's coat. "You don't think that was accidental, do you?"

He got to his feet, favoring his side again, and reached down to help her up.

"No, I don't. Someone has a serious bone to pick with one of us, and I don't mean Sugar-Bear."

Yeah, that's what she was afraid he'd say.

Chapter 19

Lucas lost track of how long he sat on the floor with Natalya's unconscious body in his arms. The fire had died down to nothing but a few glowing coals leaving a damp chill to the air, and still there was no sign of her recovering. What sort of God allows the innocent to suffer while the unjust prosper?

The anger raging inside turned into a rampant beast. It filled every pore, leaching into his soul. The longer they sat there alone, the more vengeance colored his thoughts.

He brushed a kiss over the tender skin of her forehead. Natalya had always been his angel. From the moment she and Scott moved into the house next door to his parents' shack, she'd been his savior. Her bubbly personality and positive attitude, no matter how poor they were, made the days lighter, brighter.

And her payment? Death and a deep dark hole where no one could reach her.

"C'mon, sweetheart, talk to me," he whispered, but her mouth remained lax. She reminded him of a porcelain doll he'd seen in a big department store window one Christmas. He'd wanted to get her for Nat so badly, but by the time he'd raised enough cash from bottle-picking and washing dishes at the

Chinese restaurant downtown, they'd sold out. So he'd used the money for some bootlegged whiskey instead. Yay, him.

He gently laid Natalya on her side and climbed to his feet, stretching to relieve the kinks, then bent and lifted her into his arms so he could carry her to the couch. Her body was slight and weighed next to nothing. It increased his fear for her recovery.

He used the same cover she'd thrown over him earlier, and wrapped her up snuggly before adding another log to the fire, teasing it to life. His gaze went to the sofa, willing her to open those beautiful blue eyes and mock him for his worries. She seemed so small, with that larger-than-life personality of hers subdued.

The sound of the door opening lifted his heart with a surge of hope. Maybe the Lord had heard his prayers after all. But no, Mike stepped through the entry and when their gazes met, Lucas was filled with a black rage. The room darkened as though his mood infiltrated its corners, filling the air with malevolent energy.

He jerked his head, indicating they should step outside. Mike hesitated, then nodded and went back the way he'd come. Lucas glanced at Nat once more and followed the other man, leaving the door ajar, just in case.

"Where'd you go?" he growled the moment he stepped off the landing.

Mike stiffened. "You my keeper, now?"

"What if I needed help, asshole," Lucas sneered. "We're supposed to be *teammates*, remember?"

"Fuck you," Mike snapped. "Maybe I needed some air after finding out my *mate* killed my fricking family."

Lucas' head snapped back. The vision of Mike's wife staring at him in horror through the windshield filled his mind until he thought it would shatter. This wasn't heaven, it was more like hell.

"Look, I know there's nothing I can say or do…"

"I think you've *done* enough, don't you?" Mike retorted. "Maybe this is His way of evening the score."

The storm that had threatened earlier broke. Just a few light drops at first, but then the pewter gray clouds opened up. They were soaked to the bone in seconds, yet neither moved. The wind picked up, sent waves crashing against the shore, and bent the trees until it seemed they would snap like toothpicks.

Lucas turned his face into the storm and accepted the bite of the rain against his skin. If only it could wash away his sins. Maybe Mike was right, maybe Natalya's accident was his penance, but why him? Why did everything good always disappear from his life? It wasn't fair.

A swirling mix of wind and rain surrounded him, snaking around his body and exploding upward. Lucas shook the gusts away, surprised to find his wings spread open on his back. He hadn't even noticed them forming this time.

"What the hell, man?" Mike stared at him like he'd grown…well, wings.

"What's your problem, you've seen these before." Lucas folded the wings against his body.

Mike shook his head. "It's not that, you dumb-ass. Look at them."

He glanced over his shoulder, and froze.

His beautiful white swan wings had transformed into the same leaden gray as the clouds.

Chapter 20

S cott helped Tracy to her feet, his side on fire. This was serious. She could've been killed tonight. If that shopping cart hadn't taken the brunt of the hit… He shuddered.

"Are you hurt?" He cataloged her disheveled clothing and wide-eyed stare, and wanted to growl. What the hell was going on?

This was when he could've used Lucas' calming influence. He was beginning to believe his celestial visit with his friend had been nothing more than a dream. But, that didn't stop him from wishing Lucas would make a reappearance. If anyone could get to the bottom of this, an angel could.

"Okay, that pissed me off," she snapped.

Whoa.

He stared at her in shocked surprise. Hadn't seen that one coming. A slow grin curled his lips and dissipated some of his tension.

"That's my girl. Go get 'em," he chuckled.

She frowned and bent to check her dog. "You smart boy, you. Thanks for warning us, Sugar-Bear. You're in for a treat when we get home."

What about him? He wanted a treat too. One green-eyed brunette to go, please.

Leaving them to their cuddling, Scott straightened the overturned cart and hoisted the bags. "Why don't you two wait by the doors and I'll bring the car around? There's no need for both of us to make the trip." And, he would feel better about her staying close to the safety of the building.

"Oh, no you don't." Tracy rose and planted her hands on her hips.

She was amazing. They'd just about become hood ornaments tonight. Yet there she stood, hair a mess, eyes sparking, torn stockings, the most beautiful woman he'd ever seen.

"Look, Trace…"

"Don't you 'look, Trace', me." She sighed, and moved to his side. Her fingers sent tingles upward from where they rested on his arm. "You may be used to playing the hero for damsels in distress, but that's not me, okay?" Her eyes were emerald green, mesmerizing in their brilliance. "I'm used to taking care of myself. I don't need coddling."

No, maybe she didn't. But that didn't mean she couldn't use someone to take the burden away. He wanted to be that someone.

He raised a hand and brushed a velvety soft cheek, reveling in her body's response. Eyelids fluttered and lips parted as though waiting for a kiss. Maybe she didn't want the fairy tale, but that didn't mean he couldn't be her prince.

He leaned down and accepted her invitation. Heaven.

Her taste reminded him of blue skies and endless meadows. Of songbirds and bubbling brooks.

147

She was his fire when he got cold and food when he was hungry. She made him weak, yet superhero strong, all with a look or a touch. And he couldn't get enough.

"Take me home with you," he whispered.

Tracy gazed at him, her eyes conflicted. "We should…"

"What? Slow down? Deny what's happening between us?" He tunneled his hand into her hair and cupped the side of her head, relieved when she leaned into the touch. "I can't. If there's anything I've learned in the past couple of weeks, it's that there are no guarantees."

He leaned forward until their foreheads touched. Until every breath was shared. Until there was no more room for misunderstandings.

"I want you."

Tracy released a shaky sigh. It was hard enough denying her feelings to herself, never mind the words of the man of her dreams. That was the whole issue though. This relationship was taking on all the characteristics of one of Scott's action movies. The question was; could she be his leading lady for however long he wanted her before the next big sensation came rolling into his life?

His body was a warm furnace, a heat she craved. His mouth against hers promised hours of pleasure. But more than that, it was the connection they shared. Even though they'd barely met, their bodies knew and welcomed each other.

Temptation.

Sugar-Bear whined and tugged on his leash. She stepped away from the six-two enticement and hugged her dog.

"Ready to see your new home, big guy?" She smiled when he wagged his tail, and glanced up in time to see Scott crossing the lot into the dark.

"What am I going to do, huh, boy?" His soft brown eyes stared up at her. "You think I should give him a chance, don't you?" He licked her hand.

"Way to take his side."

The rumble of the Mustang's engine warned her that she better make up her mind soon. The car pulled up and Scott leaned over to open the door for her. "Ready?" he asked.

Now, or never.

She let the dog in first, then straightened her seat and climbed in. Before she could second-guess herself, Tracy kissed Scott. She put everything she had behind that kiss. It wasn't neat, and it wasn't pretty, but it obviously got the message across. He froze. And just when she was going to pull back, embarrassed, his mouth opened over hers and she forgot to breathe.

His mobile lips tormented and teased while his tongue made her think wicked, wanton thoughts.

She squirmed and tried to get closer but only succeeded in knocking the car out of gear.

Scott pulled back at the harsh grinding sound and heaved a loud frustrated sigh.

Tracy met his gaze and smiled. "They always make love scenes in a car seem sexy."

After a moment, his lips quirked upward. "Believe me, with you, they are."

Oh, wow.

"The answer's yes, Anderson. You don't need to sweet-talk me." She couldn't meet his gaze any more and fiddled with her skirt instead.

"Hey," he said, quietly.

When she looked up he ran a light finger along her jaw and shivers popped out in its wake.

"It's not a line, okay?" He waited until she hesitantly nodded. "I want us to be together, but only if you're ready. I can wait."

She considered him doubtfully and he grinned.

"What? You don't believe I can hold on to my virtue?" He pretended to look pained, and she had to laugh.

"You don't have to," she said. And then she turned serious, though her heart was ping-ponging around her chest. "Take me home, Scott."

He gazed at her for a long moment, then gave a sharp nod, and shifted the car back into gear.

Chapter 21

Tracy awoke and stretched contentedly. The warm male body against her back explained why every bone in her body felt like butter left out in the sun. Slowly, afraid to move in case she woke him, she rolled to the edge of the bed and crawled out from beneath the down comforter.

The view when she turned would live on in her fantasies for years to follow. Scott lay spread-eagle, his big body taking up most of her king-sized mattress. The blanket had pooled on the small of his back, hinting at the globes of his drool-worthy butt. His arms tucked up under the pillow beneath his head highlighted the v-shape of his spine and the fluid lines of muscle. The black and blue bruising along his side and the white of the plaster were a stark contrast to the teak cast of his skin. Sympathy held hands with the sensuality flowing through her body.

She fought an argument with herself and turned away from the temptation. The mirror in the bathroom told the tale of their erotic encounter. She lifted her hair on top her head and shivered in remembrance of how the love marks came to decorate her neck and breasts. Her nipples hardened and her womanhood pulsed with remembered delight. The man knew how to please a woman, there was no doubt about that. But the thought of how he'd learned those skills cooled her ardor. She sighed, and turned away to climb into the shower.

The cool water made her gasp and she hurried to add more hot, relaxing as steam filled the cubicle. She'd just added citrus-scented shampoo to her hair when the glass door slid back and Scott joined her, a plastic garbage bag tied around his cast.

Unaccountably shy, Tracy got an eyeful of all that blessed-by-God body and ducked her head.

"Good morning," she murmured, scrubbing her scalp raw.

He reached out and lifted her chin, stilling her movement. The warm, teasing glow in his eyes made her lips quirk in an answering smile.

"Morning," he rasped, just before their lips met in a lingering morning-after-and-I-feel-good kiss. "Why didn't you wake me?"

The water dripped off their lashes and turned the scene surreal. How could she explain how out of depth she was? Where this was little more than a casual hook-up to him, for her... well, it wasn't. She didn't do casual. Had never had an interest in sex for pleasure's sake. Though after last night, she could see the attraction.

"Scott..."

He leaned back a little so that he could meet her eyes. "That better be a *Scott, when can we do this again?*" His gaze turned somber. "That's not what you were going to say though, was it?"

Oh God, this was hard. How was she supposed to explain that the most momentous night of her life scared her to death?

"I think we should take some time to evaluate," she started.

His expression turned inscrutable.

"Evaluate what?" he asked, and picked up where she'd left off with the scrubbing. His big hand massaging her hair made her eyes practically roll back in her head. Then they left her scalp to begin a reunion tour of her body and she was lost. The combination of slippery soap and calloused fingers had her pulse pounding so loud she barely heard what he was saying.

"What do you think this is, doc? I'm not giving up, if that's what you want." He punctuated the words with kisses that teased and promised without delivering. It drove her mad.

She rubbed against him, desperate for the friction caused by their wet bodies. Her hand slid between them and wrapped around his erection. She smiled wickedly at his answering groan, and began a slow squeeze designed to drive him around the bend. It was good, but not enough. She needed to taste him, to feel his length within her mouth. His hands forced her head back so he could meet her gaze as she fell to her knees.

"You don't need to prove anything to me," he grated.

Embarrassed, she leaned back. "Don't you like it?"

His laugh was low, pained. "God yes, but that's not the point."

Reassured, Tracy smiled a cat's smile and leaned in for a long slow lick. "What is then?"

"Oh, fuck," he groaned.

She laughed. "Well yeah, that too, I hope."

And then she made it her mission to blow his mind.

Scott lay on his side and stared at the woman sleeping next to him. Her hair, wet when they'd left the shower, now lay in a tangled coffee-colored mess across her pillow. There were marks on her smooth flesh, marks he'd placed there. Was it wrong to go all caveman and thump his chest?

She'd surprised him in the shower. His dick jumped just thinking about it. He'd never seen anything more sensual in his life. Her eyelids had slowly closed over clover green eyes dark with hunger, and then she'd proceeded to tug the heart from his soul with that greedy little mouth. He'd never be able to climb into a shower again without reliving that moment, so help him God.

When he thought of how close he'd come to losing her tonight… He brushed a stray lock of hair off her cheek and smiled when she leaned into his touch. Her body accepted him, now if he could only get that stubborn mind of hers to believe in them.

His cell set up a faint ringing from the other room where he'd dropped his jacket last night. Tracy's brows furrowed, and he cursed the thing. Careful not to jostle her, he rolled out of bed, grabbed his pants, and hurried down the hall. And of course the stupid phone shut down just before he got to it. The call display listed five missed calls from his agent. Whoops. Guess he must have been otherwise occupied. He commandoed his jeans and flopped into a flowered recliner that was more comfort than fashion before doing a callback.

"What's up?" he asked impatiently. What part of *give him some space* did the guy not get?

"Hey, man, where you been? I've been calling for hours. You bumping some bimbo, or something?" Ray's nasally, frankly annoying voice whined in his ear.

Scott glared at the framed print of a farmhouse on the opposite wall.

"Watch your mouth, I won't tell you again. What I do on my time has nothing to do with you." If he still smoked he'd be reaching for a cigarette right now. They were coming to a parting of the ways, him and ol' Ray. It was different when Lucas was alive, the agent never ran his mouth around him. Not sure why he figured it was okay now, but Scott was getting right sick of it.

"Relax, man, I didn't mean nothing. You want to screw every chick between here and L.A. it don't make no difference to me. I just want you back to work. I got some prime opportunities lined up, but they want answers like yesterday, man. Cut me a break, I'm only doing my job here. I'm sorry about Lucas, but…" Ray paused. Scott's hand fisted and he longed to punch something. "It's over, buddy. We have to move on, you get me?"

Yeah, he *got* him all right. The asshole had a gambling problem. They'd warned him about it before, but it sounded as though he was in deep again.

"Look, I have to go. I'll call you later and we'll get together to talk. I want to make some changes." He could practically hear the sweat break out on the dude's forehead.

"Let's not do anything hasty," Ray back-pedaled. "Take your time, man. There's no rush."

Scott's lips quirked cynically. "Yeah, sure, whatever. Talk to ya later." He thumbed the end button and threw the phone down on the table, wincing as it clattered. He cocked his head and listened, but all stayed silent down the hall. Good. She needed the rest.

He leaned his head against the back of her butt-ugly chair and stared at the popcorn stippling on the ceiling. The conversation with Ray wasn't going to be easy. The three of them had been a team for a lot of great years. But he was different now, they both were. With Lucas gone, the glue that bound them together was slowly stripping away. And besides, he wasn't sure he wanted to continue acting any more. It would take him away from Tracy, and he wasn't prepared to do that. He didn't need the money; he and Lucas had set up an account long ago. They funneled a good portion of their revenue into its coffers. The dream had been to take care of the two of them and Natalya so they'd never have to worry again.

If only they'd known to beware of what you wish for.

Chapter 22

That son-of-a-bitch was going to be sorry.

Ray looked at the now silent cell phone in his fisted hand. His fingers whitened around the damn thing until he half expected to see indents in the cover. His anger rose along with his blood pressure until it exploded and he threw the mobile across the room and felt a burst of satisfaction when it smashed against the wall.

It was a short-lived gratification.

What was he going to do now? The people after him weren't going to wait much longer. He limped across to the phone and grimaced at the cracked screen. More money he couldn't afford to spend. The shag rug was crunchy under his shoes. He hated to guess what lived in the chenille bedspread. This piece-of-crap room was all he could afford after his bookie's goons roughed him up a week ago and took every cent he had. They had found out his money-well was threatened by the death of his biggest star and they weren't happy.

It was all bullshit. He'd worked his ass off for those two thankless idiots and this was his reward? They raked in the cash, babes, and accolades while he got the run-around.

He'd warned Lucas more than once that they would be nothing without him and the idiot had laughed him off. He'd shown him. Who was laughing now?

Except there was a chance the medical examiner's office would find out what he'd done. He couldn't allow that. It had been easier than expected to get rid of the doctor, one pop to the head and it was over. That's what he should've done with the woman too since she was a slow learner. The warning notes, the injured dog, the hit and run, nothing seemed to stop her. And now she was screwing Anderson; yeah, he'd heard that satisfied note in his old buddy's voice.

This was all her fault. If she had just signed off on the case, he could've talked Scott into going home to L.A. so they could get their lives back on track.

But no, that bitch had to screw everything up.

It was only a matter of time before they found the fentanyl in Lucas' system; after that it wouldn't take long to trace it back to him. He'd screwed up by using his own prescription. An overdose of heroin would have worked just as well.

Ray was sorry he'd ever suggested this gig. They'd been doing fine out west. He'd gotten greedy, and it was costing him big time. It was a tough decision to get rid of Lucas, he'd thought of the kid as a son. But there'd been no choice after he threatened to press charges when he found out about the stolen money. Ray couldn't have that, it would've ruined him.

Sometimes sacrifices had to be made.

He popped the top on the bottle of whiskey and took a shot, grimacing at the cheap perfume taste. Couldn't even afford good booze any more, *shit*.

He needed a plan. Something to get Scott back to work before those goons came back and busted his kneecaps. The key was the doc; get rid of her and things would get back to normal.

They had to.

Chapter 23

Lucas glared at his sodden gray wings. What did it mean? Why was he being forsaken this way? How was he supposed to get a second chance if he couldn't even help those he cared about the most?

"You better knock that chip off your shoulder, buddy, before you mess things up good," Mike warned.

"Yeah, and what do you know about it?" Lucas growled. A shaft of light split the clouds in half and highlighted the iridescent glitter of the other angel's wings. It made him wish for his Ray-Bans. "You get lost in a tinsel factory or something?"

Mike looked at him like he'd lost his marbles. "Look, I think you should take this as a warning. Someone up here…" Mike glanced around as though the Lord would suddenly appear on that nimbus of light over their heads. "…doesn't like your attitude."

"Yeah, well, I'm not real thrilled with His right now either." Lucas stared at the house and willed Natalya to appear in the doorway.

Mike picked up a couple of flat rocks and sent them skimming the surface of the lake. It made Lucas uncomfortably aware of his life. He felt like those stones; gliding along without really accomplishing anything worthwhile.

"I'm sorry about your girlfriend," Mike said, turning to face him again.

He nodded. "Now what?" Hopefully the angel had some idea of where to go from here, because he sure didn't.

"I'm guessing you need to go back to earth and prove yourself."

Sure, no problem. Just hop the next moonbeam and sayonara. And even if he could figure out how to go back, what was he supposed to do when he got there? This do-good crap should come with a manual.

He pointed at the other man's wings. "It looks as though you already earned your hall pass, so what are you still doing here?"

Mike shrugged, his green eyes unfathomable. "It's not my time. I have a job to do, same as you."

Lucas couldn't see why, the guy had already been through hell and back, you'd think it'd be enough. He didn't give a shit if he made it to the other side or not, but Natalya deserved to, and he planned to do whatever was necessary to make it happen.

He glanced back at the little cottage again.

"Okay, let's do this."

The next time Tracy opened her eyes, it was to the delicious aroma of fresh-brewed Columbian and something that made her tummy do a happy dance. Bacon.

She smiled.

He'd stayed. And he cooked.

It was kind of hard to control the warm fuzzies, and after the night they'd shared, she wasn't sure she wanted to. Maybe, instead of over-thinking their affair, she should just enjoy it for however long it lasted. Hank had told her more than once, *"If you want something from a relationship, you have to be willing to get your feet wet."* She hadn't understood him at the time, but now it made more sense. If she wasn't willing to give anything to the relationship, then why should she expect Scott to?

She hurried through a second shower, shivering slightly as the warm water caressed her sensitized flesh. Not wanting to bother with getting fully dressed, she grabbed Scott's discarded chambray shirt and tugged it on, reveling in its softness. The hem ended at a respectable mid-thigh, but the sleeves were a mile too long. She rolled them up and followed her nose down the hall.

Entering the kitchen, she had to smile. He stood in front of the stove shirtless, spatula in hand, and a cloud of steam billowing upward.

"Are you burning our breakfast?" she teased.

He swung around and she lost her train of thought. Holy moly, the man had a fine body. His abs were delineated and accented a narrow ribbon of dark blond hair that arrowed down to her happy place. She caught sight of the undone button on his jeans and her gaze jumped to his face. He seemed just as stunned to see her and she self-consciously tugged at the hemline of her impromptu dress.

The smoke thickened and they both started to cough. Scott turned back to the burner and shoved the pan off the heat. Tracy went to give him a hand, but he waved her back.

"I've got this, just relax. Coffee is made."

She hesitated, then shrugged and poured them each a cup, carrying it over to the butcher block table. Probably not his usual décor but she liked it. Battling her insecurities, she took a drink and watched him work. Even with the cast he was amazingly dexterous—a vision of him holding himself above her with one hand planted by her head while he brought her to soul-stealing pleasure made her cheeks feel like they were the ones on fire, not the bacon.

He found a couple of mismatched Corningware plates, loaded them up, and transported them to the table with an I-told-you-I-totally-had-it-under-control look delivered from under a sexy fringe of messed up hair that made her want to run her fingers through the ends. Forget about the meal, she'd like to fill up on another kind of food entirely, the lovin' kind.

She gazed dubiously at the charred toast, blackened bacon, and rubberized scrambled eggs. "This looks wonderful," she fibbed.

Scott pulled up a chair and joined her, his grin self-depreciating. "Yeah, it sucks. Do I get points for trying though?"

Oh yeah, big points.

"We'll see. Who's in charge of cleanup?" She grinned.

"I was told whoever does the cooking is exempt from cleaning," he said, and grimaced at the hunk of egg dangling off his fork. "Next time I'll order something in."

Next time.

Her heart jumped and her stomach somersaulted—and not because of the food. She watched as he picked his way through the least offensive bits and drank her coffee with relish. Almost like they were a... couple. All they needed was a paper so he could read the sports and she could do crosswords. Crazy.

She cleared her throat. "So what are your plans for today?" *Honey.*

He eyed her over the rim of his cup. "Well, I..." A whining at the back door cut off whatever he'd been about to say.

Shoot, she hadn't even thought about letting Sugar-Bear out. Tracy jumped up before Scott could move and opened the door for her dog.

"Good morning, sweetheart. How do you like your new digs?"

Scott murmured over top the animal's happy whine. "I like it... a lot."

Flustered, she brushed her hair behind her ear and reached for a piece of the bacon on her plate, intending a peace-offering to the dog, but Scott grabbed her hand and tugged her close.

"It's true, you know." He used his thumb to tip her chin up so that she had to meet his gaze. "I really do like your home. It's warm and welcoming, just like you."

Or an old pair of shoes.

She'd been deluding herself. Why was a man who could have basically any woman on the planet going to tie himself to someone who was... comfortable?

She gave him a quick peck and pulled free. "I better get dressed. I'd like to get into the office for a while today." *And gain some much-needed perspective.*

His brows lowered. "Do you think that's a good idea? It's only been a couple days since you lost your friend."

She gave a brittle laugh. "I think I know when my partner was murdered. That's all the more reason to be there. I want to find out what the hell happened."

Ignoring his hurt look she spun away and hurried down the hall, admitting to herself she was as reluctant to shed the image of them as a couple as she was to get rid of his shirt.

Chapter 24

Leaves formed a brightly colored carpet on the sidewalk, the breeze twirling them into little piles that crunched and crackled under foot. The sky was a brilliant blue, so vivid it hurt the eyes. It felt strange entering the Medical Examiner's building from the front, but Tracy wasn't prepared to park in her usual spot underground. Too much had changed in such a short time. She nodded to people she knew, but didn't stop to chat. The last thing she wanted to do was feed their curiosity—well-meant or otherwise.

The office was thankfully empty. She shrugged off her jacket and set her purse down, all the while staring at the files waiting on her desk.

The first folder contained toxicology reports on Lucas Carmichael. She'd expected the alcohol given the booze found in the car, but it was a relief to see he'd been well under the required limit for driving. Her brow furrowed when she read the next line; trace amounts of fentanyl. What would Lucas be doing with an opiate in his system?

She rocked back in her seat and rubbed her chin. It was possible he had a prescription for the drug if he'd been injured or had surgery, but there was no evidence to support the claim. It was sometimes prescribed to patients with extreme chronic pain, but again, no sign of that either. And besides, surely Scott would've mentioned something to her, he had to know she would find it during the autopsy. It would certainly better explain why Lucas had drifted over the center line into oncoming traffic; his sense of perception would have been hampered by the drug moving through his system.

She opened the file containing pictures of the body and combed through until she found what she was looking for; he'd been wearing a patch at the time of the crash. Now that she thought about it, Tracy remembered reading something about Lucas' ongoing struggle to stop smoking. She would be willing to bet her next paycheck that she'd just found how the drug had been administered, but now the question became; by who?

She kept coming back to Scott sitting in this office and swearing that he and Lucas had nothing to do with the drug scene. What if he'd been lying to her? What if Lucas knew exactly what he'd been taking at the time of the accident? Maybe the whole quitting smoking thing was nothing more than a cover up to explain the patch. Maybe Lucas Carmichael, one half of Hollywood's dream-team, was in fact an addict who caused the horrific crash that ended in three deaths.

She slammed the file closed and put her head in her hands. She'd been played by a player. It all made a dreadful kind of sense. No wonder Scott didn't want her coming to the office, he was scared she'd figure this out. When the press got wind of the story, his career would be over. It didn't matter that he wasn't behind the wheel, he would still be deemed an accomplice. He may even be facing jail time. The courts were sure to go after vehicular manslaughter charges and probably punitive damages to the family of the driver of the van.

Tracy wished Hank were here. She could sure use his dry wit about now, even if it was aimed at her gullibility. She still couldn't believe he'd been shot. How horrifying. And here she was, upset over a little betrayal. Seemed pretty frivolous in comparison.

The best thing she could do for herself would be to turn over her findings to her boss and let him deal with the fallout while she found a nice little hole to bury herself in until it all died down and Scott Anderson became nothing more than a painful memory.

Scott wasn't sure what kind of burr had gotten under Tracy's stubborn hide, but it hadn't taken her long to send him packing this morning. Good thing he had a big enough ego or she might have trampled the thing into the ground.

He'd never told a woman he cared before. Now he knew why. The self-doubt was killing him. Had he read her wrong? Was she just in it for a fling with a movie star? It wouldn't be the first time. There were lots of chicks out there that only showed their *devotion* by the size of a guy's wallet. He hadn't taken Tracy for one of them, but what did he know? Lucas had preached often enough that money could buy just about anything, even love. Maybe he was right.

Restless, Scott drifted aimlessly for a couple of hours and then found himself in the vicinity of the park where he'd had his vision a couple of nights earlier. He wasn't sure what he expected to find; a sign maybe, some kind of proof positive that he wasn't going crazy and yes, he really had seen a ghost. Or angel. Or whatever the hell it was.

But as he followed the ribbon of walkway from one end to the other everything looked—normal. Teens, their eyes down, staring at the twenty-first century's idea of socializing they carried in their hands. Couples in love meandered along the path hand-in-hand, some young, some old. All made his chest hurt and he turned away before he started something dumb, like searching for a woman who wasn't likely to show up with an apology on her lips.

The gazebo came into view, the pristine white paint a perfect counterpoint to the day's brilliant blue skies. The trees were shedding their summer foliage, filling the lush green grass with a carpet of reds and oranges that danced and played like a bunch of woodland sprites.

Shaking his head at his fanciful notions, Scott strode up the steps and entered the structure. He wasn't sure what he expected to find, but it wasn't the tow-headed boy asleep on the wicker chair in a set of torn and dirty dinosaur pajamas.

He glanced around outside but there were no distraught parents desperately searching for their missing child that he could see. His first instinct was to call the cops, but he hesitated. Maybe there was a reason the kid had run away. What if it were an abusive home and Scott helped to place him right back in there? Memories of his own scrapes stayed his hand. Better to wait and get the boy's side of the story first.

The kid shivered and let out a little hiccupping sigh that suggested he'd cried himself to sleep. Scott frowned and tugged his jacket off before dropping it gently over the child. What now? He should probably wake him up, but another hour wouldn't make that much difference one way or the other.

Maybe Tracy could help.

His fingers had her speed-dialed practically before the thought finished processing. *Pathetic, man. You are seriously pathetic.*

"Hello?" Her voice was cautious and Scott cursed under his breath. He'd forgotten to tell her he'd helped himself to her cell number— for emergencies.

Stalker much?

"Hey, it's me. Scott." Okay, like she wouldn't recognize the voice of the guy she'd just spent the night with. *Get a grip, dude.* "Listen, I know you're probably busy with, ah… dead bodies or whatever, but I was kinda wondering if you could take a break and meet me at the park on Hillside? There's something I want you to see."

There was a long stretch of nothing and he looked at the bars on his phone, yep, what do you know, full connection.

Bringing the thing back to his ear he was just about to make some kind of lame excuse, *"Sorry, gotta go, aliens just landed, and they're looking for me,"* when she finally, finally cleared her throat and answered him.

"Yeah, sure. I had something I wanted to show you too. I'll be there soon." Click.

So, no, *"Hi, honey, I'm so glad you called. I've missed you in the three-point-five hours we've been apart. I can't wait until we're together again."*

At least she was coming. He'd take what he could get.

Chapter 25

Tracy cursed her gullibility throughout the twenty-minute drive to Hillside Park. One phone call from Scott and she was on the run, almost like she was scared he'd change his mind and tell her their affair had been a big mistake if she didn't do as he asked. She might as well admit it; when it came to Scott Anderson, she had no backbone.

She adjusted her sunglasses, grateful she'd remembered them to protect against both the bright October sunshine and a certain man's all-seeing eyes. At least traffic was fairly light. It gave her more time to question her findings before she confronted him with something she wouldn't be able to take back later. At the moment it was little more than unsubstantiated evidence, so unless he confessed, or she found something a lot more concrete than a hunch, the prosecutors had nothing to take him to trial with.

Which was her big excuse for agreeing to meet him today—or so she told herself. Tracy reached down and nervously fingered the digital recorder she'd grabbed from the lab. She was no amateur sleuth. She'd be lucky if this whole thing didn't blow up in her face.

And what if she were right?

Did she actually intend to turn States evidence on her lover?

Gah. Her stomach was a mess of knots and her heart was threatening to jump ship and leave her to sort out her own screwed up head.

The turn to the park came sooner than she would've liked. She signaled and turned into the parking lot, her gaze skimming the cars until they came to rest on Scott's Mustang. She had to fight the urge to whip a U-turn and leave before she destroyed the one really good thing in her life.

She pulled into a nearby spot and shut off her car's engine. It was her job to find out the truth whether she liked it or not. The sooner she got this over with, the sooner she'd find out if Scott really cared, or if it had all just been a sick game for him.

She turned the recorder on and hid it deep in her cross-body bag, gathered up the files she'd brought to prove her point, and climbed out of the car feeling as though she were headed for the gallows.

The couples wandering the paths in the warmth of the sun were an insult to her mood. They only showed her everything she was in danger of throwing away. Maybe, just this once, she could let sleeping dogs lay. What was done, was done. Nothing was going to bring that family their father back. Indeed, she might even make everything worse by bringing it all up again just when they'd begun the healing process.

Her steps dragging, she rounded a corner in the path and then it was too late.

Scott had been sitting on the steps of a classic white gazebo, staring at the phone in his hand as though willing the thing to ring. She must have made a sound because he glanced up and stilled. A relieved smile lit his face and showed off his sexy dimple. *Damn him.*

He stood and started down the steps, but then hesitated and glanced over his shoulder a moment, before continuing to her side.

"Hi. I was worried about you," he said.

Her curiosity at his behavior went by the wayside when he tugged her close and lowered that perfect mouth to hers. She had to concentrate to hang onto the file when all she really wanted was to wrap her arms around his neck and never let go.

"What took you so long?" he whispered, feathering distracting kisses from her brow to her chin.

"Tr...traffic," she muttered, not willing to give up the moment just yet. His hair seemed touched by the Gods in this lighting; an antique gold shot through with chartreuse. With his jacket missing, his shoulders seemed impossibly broad, highlighting a thick neck and prominent Adam's apple. She ached to lean in and nibble him there. See if he tasted half as decadent as he looked.

"You need to quit staring at me like that or I can't be held accountable for what comes next," he said, his voice little more than a growl.

Warmth flowed through her veins. He desired her, it was there in the flush of his cheeks, the heat in his eyes, and the hard length brushing up against her belly. The urge to throw the files along with the recorder into a garbage can and take her man deep into the forest where no one would find them was overwhelming.

But then reality intruded.

"Hey, mister. This your coat?"

Tracy jumped back as though scalded.

A young boy stood where Scott had been sitting, his hair rumpled and expression nervous.

"Friend of yours?" she asked, lifting her chin toward the child, and hugging the file to her chest.

Scott gazed at her clutching those papers and his face turned inscrutable. "What's going on, Trace?"

That was the million-dollar question of the day, wasn't it?

"Later." She stepped around him and moved toward the stairs. "Why don't you introduce me to your young friend?"

The kid didn't look to be more than eight or nine. Red-blond hair stuck up in tufts around a dirty, freckled face. He wore dinosaur pj's which seemed kind of strange, but then, what did she know about what kids were into wearing these days?

Scott came up beside her and said under his breath, "That's why I called. I think he's in trouble, or something." Then, to the kid, "You better keep my coat for now, it's kind of chilly out here. This is

Tracy, she's a friend. I asked her to come 'cause I get lonely sometimes."

Tracy's heart squeezed as his gaze skimmed over her with warm blue eyes, then he edged a few steps closer to the child. "How about you, buddy? Where's your family?"

The boy's eyes flashed fear and he backed up into the gazebo. "I'm not s'posed to talk to strangers."

"Well, that's certainly true," Scott reassured him. "But we're not really strangers any more, are we? You have my coat."

"Scott," Tracy warned.

He glanced back. "I'm just trying to…"

"Look out," she cried as the boy took advantage of the moment, dropped the jacket, and leaped down the stairs. He froze, looked up at Scott with eyes that filled his whole face, then spun and took off across the park heading for a thick stand of spruce trees.

Tracy exchanged a startled look with Scott, then they broke into a trot and followed after the child.

"Wait, we don't want to hurt you," she called. "We just want to help you." The kid wasn't buying it though, he disappeared into the forest faster than she would've thought those little legs could go.

"That went well," Scott grunted, and Tracy could tell his ribs were taking a beating.

"Why don't you wait here and I'll find him," she offered.

He gave her a get-real glance.

"Yeah, I didn't think so," she gasped.

177

They crashed through the undergrowth like a herd of buffalo and Tracy wasn't too surprised when they didn't see any sign of dinosaur tracks.

"Who is he?" she asked when they finally stopped for breath.

Scott hunched over and held his side. "Not sure. I found him sleeping back there. Should've just called the cops."

"Why didn't you?"

He shrugged. "I figured maybe you could talk to him first. Make sure he's not from an abusive family, or some shit."

Something in Scott's expression told Tracy more than he probably wanted her to know. She'd read somewhere before that he and Lucas came from a poor background. She sensed it had also been a rough upbringing. Her eyes teared for the boy who'd grown into the successful, driven man standing before her now.

She was in love with him.

And why that should surprise her she didn't know. He had so many admirable qualities; how she'd ever doubted him was a mystery. He'd done nothing but care for her since the moment they'd met. Someone with characteristics like that—those of a natural care-giver—would never deliberately hurt another human being. She had it all wrong. The relief was sweet.

"What are you smiling about?" His voice made her jump and she dropped the file. Of course the wind picked that moment to escalate and carried the pages topsy-turvy into the brush.

"Oh no," she cried. The last thing she wanted was some kid finding pictures of Lucas Carmichael laid out in a morgue.

She swore under her breath and chased after the quickly disappearing papers. One caught in a bramble patch and she scraped the back of her hand yanking it out. She hissed and shook her hand to relieve the sting. Just as she was about to turn away in search of more, a scrap of white caught her attention.

Tracy crouched for a better view.

A set of wide, frightened eyes stared back.

"Hey, you had us scared. Are you okay?"

It took a few hold-her-breath moments, but he finally nodded, and she sighed her relief. "Good. Okay, we're going to get you out of there. Just hang on, buddy, it won't be long."

Tracy stood and turned excitedly, "Scott, I fou…"

Scott was staring at her like he didn't even know her. "What the fuck is this?" He waved a sheaf of papers in the air and Tracy could see her yellow post-it notes floating in the breeze.

"I can explain," she whispered, her stomach dropping through her shoes.

His laugh wasn't pretty. Actually it was downright terrifying.

Chapter 26

Scott looked down at the tattered remnants of paper clenched in his hand and saw only shattered dreams. In thirty-two years of hard living he'd never felt as gutted as he did right now. How was it even possible that he could still breathe? The pain was indescribable. The betrayal unimaginable.

"Scott," Tracy pleaded, her lying green eyes soft with regret.

He decided to walk away before he said something he might regret and almost dared her to follow. To give him an outlet for the anger churning inside. Snapshots of their time together flitted through his mind, driving a spike to his heart. How could she believe he would cover up such a duplicitous act? Even if it were true, which it sure as fuck wasn't, he would never condone driving while under the influence. What did she take them for? Lucas wasn't like that—and neither was he.

According to her little *investigation*, she'd decided guilty until proven innocent. This was such bullshit. She could have, should have, talked to him about her suspicions. Instead, she'd decided to pull judge and jury without a fair trial.

Un-freaking believable.

How could he have been so stupid?

As he neared the gazebo, Scott noticed his discarded jacket and it brought him up short. Shit, he was supposed to be finding that poor kid. He couldn't just leave. Much as it grated to have to see her again right now, he'd better go back and join the search. But first he needed to call Ray to set him up with a lawyer.

"So you're ready to get back to work? That's great, man. I've got a line on a new action film being shot in Panama. What do you think?" Ray's nasally twang reverberated in his ear.

"Hi, Ray, yeah, I'm great. And you?" Sarcasm dripped from Scott's voice, but he didn't care. The guy could take a second for common pleasantries, couldn't he?

Ray choked out an ingratiating laugh. "Sorry, man. Just excited to be getting back to work, that's all."

Scott frowned. Why had he never noticed how desperate his agent sounded before? Maybe it had to do with losing his sister and Lucas, but suddenly everything to do with that lifestyle seemed repulsive. It was little more than a rat-race between the publicity and never-ending fitness regimes in order to stay at the top of the lists. He was tired of it.

"We'll talk about that later. Right now I need you to find me a good lawyer." He waited for the other shoe to drop...

"What? Haven't you gotten yourself into enough shit for awhile?" Ray sputtered. "I barely managed to keep a lid on the last episode. C'mon, man, you're killing me here."

And there it fell.

Scott inhaled a harsh breath and noticed the vapor when it released. It was cooling down quick. Time to find the kid. "I gotta go. Just get me a name, okay? Can you handle that?" He thumbed the phone to off and shoved it into the back pocket of his jeans before reaching for his coat. Tracy would need it, she only had a light shirt on. And why he cared about that, he was damned if he knew.

Annoyed, and more than a little frustrated with a green-eyed brunette, he turned and retraced his path back into the woods. It had grown considerably darker, the canopy above blocking both light and sound. Everything was muted, the traffic, the sunlight, even the cries of unseen birds in the trees. There'd been a forest not far from their trailer when he'd been growing up. He and Lucas spent a lot of time there; building tree forts and imaginary worlds where they were the rulers instead of the servants. He remembered Natalya scaring the hell out of them one time. She'd been sent to bring him and Lucas home, but instead she got turned around and lost her way. Scott wasn't sure what his mom had been thinking; Nat was only four years old. By the time the boys found her, hidden in a briar patch, she'd been scratched, bleeding, and petrified. She would only settle down after Lucas took her in his arms and rocked her.

Funny, he'd forgotten that until now.

Pine needles crunched under his feet, sending up a pungent scent that reminded him of the hospital. He rubbed the cast and hoped it wouldn't hamper the search efforts. He must be close, but there was no sign of either Tracy or the boy.

"Traceeey," he called, and didn't want to admit to the worry that clouded his tone. "Hell… lloooo."

He stopped moving and listened, but only silence answered him.

Maybe she'd found the child and walked out already. But if that were the case he should have run into her, there was only the one path that he knew about.

His gaze searched the shadows, desperate for some hint of movement, something to tell him a direction to take.

And then he saw it.

The wind had kicked up again, the trees swaying like lovers dancing a waltz. A piece of paper floated up, then down, a victim of the currents, and Scott lunged. It was a copy of the forensic report. The one he'd read earlier with Tracy's notes along the side. The one that labeled Lucas with negligence and him as an accomplice.

He crumpled it in his hand and pushed it into his pocket, instead of ripping it to shreds as he would have liked. At least it gave him a direction; deeper into the forest.

Tracy trudged through the brush, wincing as branches poked and scratched her tender skin. It had begun to drizzle about ten minutes ago and she was already soaked. And cold. If she'd known, she would be spending the night in the woods she could have changed into some all-weather clothes instead of her flimsy suit.

She shivered and hugged herself for warmth. That poor kid. If she was this cold she hated to think how he was feeling in nothing more than a pair of cotton pajamas. If only she and Scott hadn't had that blow-out. They'd scared him with their yelling and he'd run the moment he could. She should probably phone the police and let them handle it, but... Scott's expression when he'd asked for her help stayed her hand. For now. But if she didn't find him soon, she wouldn't have a choice; night was coming.

If only Scott had given her time to explain. The more Tracy thought about it, the more she realized she'd gotten it all wrong. She'd jumped to conclusions because her own insecurities had led her down that road. There had to be another answer and she planned on finding out what that was; as soon as she located Scott's missing child.

She broke through a tangle of bushes and nearly slipped into a creek. The water was high thanks to the recent rains they'd had, almost cresting the steep banks and Tracy's stomach rolled. Panic set in. She frantically scanned the banks looking for those silly dinosaur pj's… and oh my God, there he was. He must have tried to cross and was caught by the current. It had swept him downstream and under some low-hanging branches.

She skidded into the water, gasping as it hit her thighs. The mud sucked at her feet, hampering her movements, but she forged on, desperate to get to the facedown body of the boy.

Don't be too late. Please, Lord, don't let me be too late.

She grabbed the branch in one hand for leverage and tugged on the sodden pajamas with the other. There was an awful moment went it didn't seem like he was going to move, but then he broke free and sent Tracy backward onto her ass, water spraying everywhere. She blinked and scrambled up, hurrying to turn him over, and cringing at the pale face and blue lips. There was no time to waste.

She leaned over that too-white face, tipped his head back, pinched his nose, and breathed into his mouth. It took a couple of tries before the kid coughed, choked, and spit up half the stream. Tracy had never been so relieved in her entire life. Guess those First Aid courses had finally paid off.

"Take it easy. I've got you," she stuttered. "You're going to be okay." Or he would be as soon as they got out of this water and into dry clothes. "Hang on to me, I'll get us out of here."

Easier said than done. The embankment was muddy and the water kept trying to knock her off her feet. The kid had a chokehold on her neck, which was good, but it made movement that much harder. Tracy was starting to worry that she wouldn't be able to get them out.

Finally, the creek widened and grew shallower, allowing her to gain a footing and climb up the bank with the help of some branches. She fell to her knees and hugged the child tight, sobbing into his shoulder now that they were safe.

"That was close," she said.

"I knew we'd make it." He leaned back and met her teary-eyed gaze. "My daddy told me so."

Looking into those innocent green eyes, the weirdest feeling came over her as light broke through the canopy of trees and bathed them in an ethereal glow. Where seconds earlier she'd been shivering and frightened, now there was only peace, and a warmth that went to the bone.

"Who's your daddy?" she whispered, though she had a feeling she already knew the answer.

"He's an angel," the boy replied.

Chapter 27

Lucas hovered near the edge of the woods and cursed his forgetfulness. The kid in the water, the one who had almost died moments ago, was the child he'd chased just after getting his wings. He was sure of it. He glanced at the grimly silent angel by his side—Mike's son.

Thank God they had arrived in time. His conscience couldn't handle more death.

"You going to talk to him? He knows you're here." The glitter from the other man's wings had lit up the entire meadow. Pretty really. Lucas tried to ignore the shadows lunging from the area he occupied.

"No. I shouldn't have said anything to him before. We're only allowed to direct their dreams, not their reality." Mike's focus remained on his oldest child. "Thanks for helping the woman to save him. I owe you." When he glanced at Lucas, his eyes were black with repressed emotion.

If only he knew.

Lucas gazed down on the little tableau and debated the wisdom of sharing his mistake with the angel. After all, it had ended well. The kid was going to be fine. No harm, no foul.

A sharp jab to the ribs, right over his heart, made him think otherwise. Apparently, he was expected to come clean. What good would it do? His and Mike's relationship was strained enough without this latest mess.

"That's not the point." The voice came from nowhere and everywhere.

Lucas shot a glance at Mike, but the angel didn't react. So—obviously aimed at him then. Okay, he could do this.

"Hey, bro," *What are you, in third grade?* "Remember when you went to see your wife a few nights back?"

Mike turned that enigmatic gaze of his on Lucas. "What about it?"

Oh yeah, this is going to be fun.

"Confession is good for the soul." That voice again.

Says who?

"Quit procrastinating."

Lucas sighed. "You're going to be pissed." He flapped his massive wings and noticed the storm clouds gathering on the horizon. "While you were inside I saw your kid jump from a window."

Mike stiffened. "And you didn't think to stop him?" His fists clenched and his body levitated a few feet into the air.

Lucas lifted his chin and glared at the other man. "Of course I did. What do you take me for?"

"Well then? You want to explain how *my son* came to be lying upside down in a muddy creek then?" Mike's voice shook the ground, there was so much rage and frustration harnessed within the chords.

Lucas checked to make sure the woman and child were okay. They were huddled under a tree and she had the boy wrapped tight in her arms.

He turned back to Mike just in time to dodge a blow to the face.

What the…?

Not taking time to ask questions, Lucas ducked and plowed into the other man's gut, driving him backward about ten feet. Mike grunted and spat phlegm to the side. He wiped his mouth with a shaking hand.

"Quit doing that," he growled. "Look, Mike, let me…"

Mike swore. "Don't you think you've done enough?" Tears shone on his cheeks and he brushed them away impatiently. "Thanks to you I've lost my family and today my son almost died. I'm tired of forgiving you, man. I wish I'd never laid eyes on you."

He gazed at his boy for a long heartbreaking minute, then he turned and took flight. The light that had bathed the meadow went with him, leaving the sky bleak and gray.

A golf ball had lodged in Lucas' throat. How was he supposed to right a wrong of this magnitude?

Rain began to fall and he looked at the two shivering on the ground. They needed shelter. Maybe there wasn't anything physical he could do to help them, but psychologically…

He fed thoughts of a warm fire and hot chocolate, love and laughter into their minds and watched as their bodies relaxed and they went off to sleep.

Now to get them some help.

Scott was worried. It was getting late and he still hadn't picked up Tracy's trail. Soon it would be too dark to properly see. He was afraid of missing a sign that would lead him in the right direction and hated to think how scared they must be, so he concentrated on searching for anything that was out of place. Broken branches, a scrap of cloth, scuffed earth. Something, there had to be a sign, he had faith.

Rain had started to fall in a steady drizzle. He prayed they had found some kind of shelter to protect themselves until he could find them, if he could figure out where the hell he was. He'd left the trail a while ago and now was hopelessly lost.

The sound of gushing water led him to a brook, half hidden by low hanging branches and willows crowding the banks. It was too wide to jump so he followed it downstream, his feet squelching through the sodden grass. A couple of times he narrowly saved himself from tripping and landing hard on his bad arm. This was a nightmare. He should never have walked away. If he didn't find them soon…

A light up ahead caught his attention. Maybe the storm was finally going to cut him a break. He hurried forward on the slippery grass, his heart unaccountably beating faster. Even when the light disappeared, leaving a dreary mist in its wake, Scott couldn't contain the burst of hope.

And then he saw them.

They were huddled together at the foot of a towering pine tree. He stopped and tipped his head to the sky. He'd never been a religious man, but this sure felt like a '*come to Jesus moment.*'

They had fallen into an exhausted slumber, and he decided to leave them rest. Scott draped his coat over their bodies and settled down to watch over them. His cell told him what he expected; no coverage. So they were on their own for getting out of here. That's okay, now that he'd found them, he wasn't going to take his eyes off them again.

Chapter 28

Tracy awoke to childish laughter. She stretched, relishing in the warmth of the leather jacket covering her from shoulder to thigh. Scott. The expensive scent of his cologne on the collar teased her senses; sweet and spicy, cardamom, patchouli, and a hint of cocoa. *Mmm*.

Full consciousness returned and she sat up in a rush, the coat pooling in her lap. Scott looked up, a smile creating a sexy dimple in his cheek.

"Hi," he murmured, his eyes warm on her face.

Embarrassed, she lowered her gaze to Dustin—he'd confessed his name after the near drowning. "How you doing, buddy?" Thankfully, he seemed fully recovered. His cheeks were pink and eyes sparkling as he squirmed under Scott's tickling fingers.

"Scott said you were *Sleeping Beauty* and he might need to kiss you to wake you up," he giggled.

She raised her eyebrow. "Maybe this princess only accepts kisses from cute little boys. What do you say to that?"

Dustin made a face. "I don't kiss *girls*," he muttered.

Scott ruffled his hair. "That's okay, sport. I got you covered." The grin he shot her way was pure devil.

Saved by the bell, Tracy's tummy grumbled. She remembered she hadn't had anything to eat since the morning's aborted breakfast with Scott. She looked at Dustin.

"You ready to go home, Dustin? Your mom and dad must be worried sick."

He tucked his chin into his chest and fiddled with Scott's casted arm wrapped around his waist. "I told you—my daddy is an angel and my mom is so sad, she won't even know I'm gone."

Oh, honey.

Her heart wept for the child who had been through so much at such a tender age. Sometimes life just wasn't fair. She looked to Scott for help, but he shook his head, either unwilling or unable to come up with the right words.

"It's okay to be sad." She cleared her throat and reached over to squeeze Dustin's knee. "I bet you're sad too, right?" She waited for his slight nod. "I think your mom would feel pretty bad if she thought you felt lonely. Maybe you just need to talk to her. What do you think?"

He rubbed his eyes and swiped his nose before meeting her gaze. "Will you come with me?"

She latched onto his hand and choked back tears of her own. "You bet. I'd love to meet your mom and tell her about the brave little man she's raised."

They sat like that for a few moments until a random shiver worked its way up Tracy's spine and she realized how chilly Dustin's fingers were. "We better get going before we're all laid up drinking chicken noodle soup for the next couple of weeks."

She hid her smile at the identical looks of dismay on their faces. Men, they were all the same. Tough as nails until they thought they were sick, then look out, they became the biggest babies on the planet.

Twilight was right around the corner and what had appeared an inviting, friendly forest now seemed dark and forbidding. She was afraid it wouldn't be easy to find their way out.

"Do you have your phone?" she asked Scott. Maybe they could use his GPS. She'd looked for hers earlier, but must have lost her cell somewhere during her mad flight.

He tugged it out of his pocket and thumbed it on, but then shook his head and pointed it her way so she could get a look. "No bars. We're on our own."

Great. A city full of cell towers and they were in the only quadrant without coverage. Figures. Well, best to put a brave face on and move to plan B then.

"How about a light?"

Scott looked at her askance for a moment, then he grinned. "Gotta love modern technology," he said, and moved through the phone's apps until he found the flashlight. Immediately their little grove was lit with high beams, shoving the shadows back to the fringe of the forest. Tracy sighed her relief and pushed to her feet.

"Okay, gang, what do you say we get out of here?"

"Yay," Dustin cried. "I'm hungry."

Tracy gave him a quick hug. "Me too. The sooner we start walking, the sooner I can buy you the best pizza you ever tasted."

Scott waved his light around the clearing. "The path can't be too far off. Let's go this way." He started toward a break in the trees. "So, what kind of pizza do you like, Dustin? My favorite is pepperoni."

Tracy appreciated his effort to keep the little guy's mind on something other than their current situation. Where the heck had all those wandering couples disappeared to now that they could use the help?

"Cheese, lots of cheese," Dustin answered, and Tracy's mouth watered.

"Me too. I'm going to buy us the biggest cheese pizza I can find when we get out of here. And a pepperoni for Scott, I guess."

Dustin giggled.

She loved the versatility of a child. One minute half-drowned, the next making jokes with virtual strangers. She was almost a basket case and it hadn't even happened to her. She didn't know what to make of his determination his father was an angel. If his dad had died… well, that was too sad to think about. Whatever the case, someone had surely been watching over him today. If she'd been even a couple of minutes later…

"Aha," Scott shouted triumphantly. The phone's little light cast a glow on the well-trodden path they'd been searching for. "Now, which way should we go?"

"This way, silly," Dustin said with absolute certainty, pointing to the right.

Tracy looked at Scott and shrugged. One way was as good as another. Eventually it had to lead them out.

Scott put the light under his chin so that he looked like a ghoulish monster. "Whatever my master decrees," he moaned, his voice dark and wobbly. Then he grinned and dropped the beam to the ground. "Sorry, couldn't resist. Okay, we'll try your way, partner. You stick in the middle; we don't want you getting lost again. Ready?"

Dustin nodded and they were off.

Tracy twisted her foot a couple of painful times on the rutted trail, and muffled her groans. Her heels were definitely not meant for search and rescue. Scott was singing campfire songs up ahead, keeping Dustin occupied so he wouldn't get scared. She'd seen a different side to him today, one that she liked—a lot. He continually surprised her. His kindness and generosity had been the first thing to draw her to him, but his humor and sensitivity were the threads that wrapped around her heart. She loved this man. More than she'd thought possible. She just hoped she hadn't come to the realization too late to make it work between them. She owed him a big apology for her misconceptions. Somehow she would make it up to him.

Her foot twisted again, and she grunted. The painful wrench made it hard to walk. She stopped for a moment to rub her swollen ankle and wished for a tensor bandage to give it some support. When she looked up Scott and Dustin were rounding a corner in the trail, the light disappearing with their bodies. Shoot, now she had to play catch-up in the dark.

She felt around the edge of the path until her fingers came across a sturdy stick to enable her to move more easily.

Angry voices up ahead sent her hurrying forward. As she rounded the bend, Tracy stumbled to a halt. Scott stood with his feet planted in the middle of the path, Dustin cowering at his back. She couldn't see the other person, but instinctively knew he was trouble. It was obvious from the tension radiating in the air.

Now what?

Chapter 29

Scott rounded a bend in the trail and saw Ray striding toward them down the path. He sighed, relieved. That is until he got a look at the gun in the other man's hand. A gun pointed straight at his heart.

"Ray, it's me, buddy. I can't believe you found us." He lifted his hands in a show of peace. "Put that thing down before you hurt someone."

Ray's laugh was humorless. "Do what I say and maybe you won't find out if I know how to shoot. Now keep them hands up there where I can see them. You and I have some business to attend to, and I'm tired of waiting while you chase after some skank who knows more than what's good for her."

Scott tensed.

What did Tracy have to do with this? The animosity in the agent's voice sent a shiver of apprehension up his spine.

"Look, I don't know what it is you need, but we can work this out. Just drop the weapon first." He widened his stance in the faint hope Ray hadn't noticed anyone was with him. And how the hell had he found him, anyway?

"I'm glad you happened along," Scott said. "I didn't know if I was ever going to get out of here."

Ray chuckled and held up his cell phone in his free hand. "I tracked you. It was hard for awhile when you dropped off the grid, but as soon as you came back on line, I had ya."

This was surreal. And more to the point, how was he going to get them out of this without anyone getting hurt? The thought of Tracy at the hands of this madman made his blood run cold.

"How long have you been following me, Ray?"

The gun wavered for a fraction of a second. "A couple of years now." Ray tilted his chin defiantly. "I had to keep an eye on my assets, didn't I?"

Scott shook his head. He couldn't believe what he was hearing. "Investments, Ray? That's all Lucas and I were to you? Freaking investments?"

"Don't you get all holier than thou with me, boy." Ray stomped closer. "I gave everything to your careers, and what did I receive in return? *'Ray, get me drink. Ray, get me a car. Ray, wipe my ass.'* I'm sick and fucking tired of being your lackey. I told Lucas I wanted more money and you know what he did? He laughed. He fucking laughed." A malicious light entered his eyes. "He ain't laughing no more though, is he?"

Was Ray saying he murdered Lucas and Natalya?

"It was an accident..." His throat was so clogged with emotion he had a hard time pushing the words out. His knees threatened to buckle. He couldn't grasp what was happening, it seemed like a nightmare. A jumbled kaleidoscope rolled through his head. Ray taking them in, making them stars, giving them more than they'd ever had in their sorry-assed lives. The cars, the houses, the women, all thanks to this man. Except he hadn't done it for them at all, he'd done it to feed his gigantic gambling addiction. Oh, he thought they didn't know he was skimming the royalties from their movies, but they'd known. And they'd let it go because he was Ray, the man who had cared enough to see something in a couple of kids from nowhere.

Ray grinned, his teeth gleaming in the shadows. "Sure, an accident I engineered. A little shot of fentanyl added to those stupid quit smoking patches he wore and he was probably having a grand ol' time behind the wheel. Guess who got the last laugh, huh?"

The fucker was dead. Enraged, Scott charged. The phone he'd been holding went flying, sending a crazy beacon of light into the air. As he connected with Ray's shoulder a spasm of pain ricocheted through his arm, and black dots leapt before his eyes. The gun hit the path and bounced.

Tracy screamed.

And then he was involved in a life and death struggle and there was no time for anything else. Ray was in better shape than he looked, the blows he landed connecting with Scott's ribs and fractured arm. But Scott had vengeance on his side, the pain numbed by his need to avenge his family.

They traded shots until both were gasping for breath, circling each other like a couple of warriors. Ray lurched for the gun at their feet, and Scott swore, too far back to stop him from reaching it first.

He turned and raced toward Tracy and the kid, "Run, he's got a gun."

A shot rang out, narrowly missing them as it kicked up rocks near their feet. Tracy picked up the boy and jumped off the path, running helter-skelter through the trees. They got about a quarter mile back in the bush when her foot twisted and she went down hard, rolling to protect Dustin. Scott followed, manhandled them up, and continued moving. There was no time to make sure they were okay, they needed to stay alive first.

Another shot blasted through the forest, this time accompanied by a searing burn to his side. Shit, he'd been hit.

Things got real after that.

"You keep running. Stay to the shadows," he wheezed. "I'm going to circle back and try to take him down."

"No," Tracy hissed. "It's too dangerous. Scott, please."

He squeezed her arm, frustrated there wasn't more he could do to keep them safe. "You'll be okay, I promise. I won't let anything happen to you." He turned her into his arms, sucking back a harsh gasp at the resulting pain.

"I love you, Tracy." He dropped his mouth to hers and tasted tears. "Don't cry, honey. We're going to make it out of here. Have faith."

A crashing noise in the bush off to their left told him he was out of time.

"Go." He pushed them away from the noise and faded into the undergrowth, stopping only long enough to make sure they were on the move, then he turned and embraced the night, becoming predator instead of prey.

Lucas gasped and hunched over, his side on fire. What the…? He'd been sitting on the bank of the creek wondering what he was supposed to do next now that he'd helped to save Mike's kid when the pain hit him. The moment he heard the report of gunfire he was on his feet. He went airborne and tried to get a handle on where the sound originated, but couldn't hear over the pounding of his heart. Scott was in danger; he knew it in the depths of his soul.

He raced over the dark landscape, a shadowy form, blending with the forest. At first there was nothing, then he caught a glimpse of white and ducked, coming in low over the boy and the woman. She seemed to have been injured, her body listing sideways as she held onto the child. They were running through the dense undergrowth of the forest, fear turning their faces a ghostly white.

Lucas landed and waited for whatever was chasing them to appear. Suddenly, a man broke cover so close to the boy that the woman shrieked. She threw up her arms to attack, but was no match for the man. He threw a sharp jab, catching her near the ear and she went down. Then he grabbed the kid and started to haul him through the bush.

Lucas reached out to stop him but his hand went right through the guy's arm. He couldn't believe there was nothing he could do to stop him. What was the use of being an angel if he couldn't help anyone?

"Humans have the freedom to choose the path they will take," the Lord said.

Lucas clenched his fists. "The kid isn't being given a choice," he growled.

"You may only shed light, my son," the Lord replied.

A light. What was a *light* going to do?

Scott appeared out of the surrounding darkness, his face grim. Lucas was so happy to see his buddy that it took a moment to realize he'd placed himself directly in the line of fire. The man stood his ground, a gun aimed at Scott's head, and his arm wrapped around the kid's neck.

Desperate to do something, Lucas flew forward, landing between the two men. Scott's eyes widened and Lucas grinned. "Happy to see me, buddy?"

"You're real. I thought it was all a dream," Scott whispered.

"What the fuck are you talking about?" the man snarled, and that's when Lucas got another shock. The man holding a gun on his best bud was none other than Ray Farrell. Talk about having the wool pulled over your eyes. Ray had been like a father to them. What the hell was going on?

"I'll explain later," Scott said, as though he'd heard the question. "Right now, I could use a hand taking care of this piece of shit."

"Shut up," Ray screeched, spittle flying out of his mouth. His hold on the kid tightened. "Shut up or I'm going to put a bullet between your eyes, money or no goddamn money."

Lucas had heard enough. His wings outstretched, he delved into the mind of his old agent, searching for a way to end this insanity. Instead, he saw the reason for his immortality and Mike's loss of a family. Sweet Jesus, this man had destroyed so many lives in search of the almighty dollar. The urge to squeeze his brain like a pimple was overwhelming.

"Do this and you are no better than him whom you seek to punish," the Lord warned.

The vengeance filling his soul demanded restitution, deafening him to God's word. Lucas applied more pressure and Ray groaned in agony. The hand holding the gun trembled and his finger pressed the trigger. The gun went off. The bullet slid right through Lucas' spirit body barely causing a ripple.

He let himself be seen and grinned the devil's smile at Ray's look of horror.

A pained grunt from Scott wiped the smirk from his lips. Lucas swung around in time to see his friend fall to the ground grasping his thigh.

His rage turned the heavens black.

"Beware, my child, for he knows not what he's done," the Lord counseled.

He swore and tightened his grip on Ray's brain, torturing in the only way he knew how.

"Lucas, stop," Scott pleaded, and finally the words sank in.

The fury slowly drained, leaving Lucas empty.

He lifted his hands and placed them on Ray's shoulders. Then he closed his eyes and prayed for his enemy.

Chapter 30

T racy crawled from the ditch and froze, not believing what her blurry eyes were seeing. She blinked hard and tried to focus on the scene playing out in front of her. Scott stood a few feet away facing the man who'd chased them through the woods. A gun was pointed at his head and Dustin dangled from under the man's arm. The poor kid was on his toes, stretched as if on a rack, his chubby fingers clawing at the forearm around his neck. Scott's phone lay on the side of the trail, the flashlight casting an eerie glow over the landscape. Trees rocked back and forth as though bearing witness to the unfolding events, and the wind and rain seemed to decide now was a good time to kick up the melodrama.

Her head felt like someone had taken a sledgehammer to it, but even that wasn't enough to explain what appeared to be the corporeal image of Lucas Carmichael, complete with a magnificent set of pigeon-gray wings, standing between the two men. A radiance emanated from the form, the rays shooting toward the heavens. Angry words she couldn't make out for the ringing in her ears were spoken, then suddenly the gun went off in an explosion of smoke and light. Scott dropped, blood soaking his jeans.

Tracy screamed again, her heart competing with the reverberations of the blast.

"Scott," she cried. "Oh my God, Scott."

She struggled to her feet and hobbled to his side, the sobs tearing her chest. The bullet had ripped through the meaty part of his thigh. The sulfur scent of the gunshot blending with the metallic odor of fresh blood turning her stomach inside out. Her teeth clattered and her hands trembled so hard she was scared she'd add to his pain, but she had to stanch the wound so she buckled down and did what needed to be done.

"You shouldn't be here," he gasped. "It's too dangerous."

"Never mind me," she answered. "You need help."

He lay on the gravel, the cords in his neck pulled taut with agony. She glanced over her shoulder at the wings of the angel and tugged her shirt over her head. Shivering in her bra, she applied it to the injury and cringed at Scott's deep moan of agony, tears making it hard to see.

"I'm sorry. I'm so, so sorry," she whispered.

"Is he going to make it?" Lucas asked, his voice startling her with its normalcy.

She looked up into a set of worried eyes and acknowledged the bond between the two men was strong. "He needs proper medical care. I'm no doctor."

Lucas gave a sharp nod, then returned his attention to the man he called Ray.

"Let the boy go, he's not part of what is between us."

Ray's voice squeaked, and Tracy almost felt sorry for the guy. Except that he'd shot the man she loved and deserved whatever the angel had in store for him.

"I let him go, then what? You going to let me go?" he whined.

"What do you think?" Lucas drawled. "What I don't understand is why you didn't just come to us if you needed help. We were your friends."

The past tense didn't go unnoticed. Ray snorted. "*Friends*. I *did* come to you, you son-of-a-bitch, and you laughed in my face. Thought it was some huge joke. I needed you, man, and you weren't there," he mumbled. "You weren't there."

Lucas' hands turned white on the other man's shoulders. "So you had me killed? All for the sake of some money? And what about the people I hit? Did you stop for one selfish second and give them a thought, you asshole?"

Dustin cried out and Tracy whirled just in time to see Ray go flying backward as though propelled from a cannon.

She opened her arms and Dustin ran into them, burying his head into her shoulder. Poor kid, he'd been through so much. They all had.

Lucas followed after Ray and stood over his crumpled body. "Get up, you bastard. Get up and accept your fate."

Ray crab-walked backward, fear turning his face into a grotesque mask. "Leave me alone, you monster."

Lucas' chuckle was harsh and vindictive. His wings arched. "Takes one to know one, old friend." He held out his hand. "C'mon, get up."

Dustin squirmed his way loose and stared in awe at the angel. "Do you know my daddy?" he asked, his voice husky from Ray's abuse.

Lucas froze. His wings stretched and quivered, seeming to have a life of their own. The dark feathers picked up a light from within, touched with moon-dust at the tips. It was the most beautiful thing Tracy had ever seen.

"Lucas," Scott begged. "Let him be. He's not worth it."

He shifted, trying to sit up, and Tracy hurried to help, scooting to the side and bracing him with her shoulder. His weight bore her forward and she could feel the dampness of blood under her fingers from his side. He needed help, and he needed it soon.

"Dustin, honey, bring me that cell phone, will you please?"

"Stay right there, kid. You're not going anywhere." Ray had risen behind Lucas and held the gun pointed at the boy.

Lucas spun, knocking the gun from Ray's hand in an impressive kick that sent the weapon flying into the brush.

"You're starting to piss me off," he growled, and grabbed him by the collar, forcing Ray to his knees. "If I were you, I'd start praying. They don't take kindly to child abusers where you're going."

He looked at Scott and grinned. Tracy could see the boys they had been in that expression. Trouble, pure trouble.

"Okay kid, you can do like the pretty lady asked now. I got this piece of sh… dirt, under control," he said.

Dustin ran over to the fading light of the phone and brought it back to Tracy. She glanced at Lucas, then dialed emergency.

"We need help. A man's been shot."

"Take it easy, ma'am," the dispatcher soothed. "Can you tell me your name and where you are located? We'll have someone there soon to help."

It only took a few moments, but it felt like a lifetime. Tracy explained the details as best she could, all the while keeping a worried eye on Scott's pasty face. When she got off the line, she leaned over and placed her lips to his, and was relieved when they softened and moved against hers.

"I love you," she whispered.

His eyes crinkled at the edge and he smiled. "About damn time."

Chapter 31

Lucas frowned at Ray's prone body.

"Why'd you do it, Ray?" He stared down at the shell of a man he'd known for half his life, when the truth was, he hadn't known him at all.

Ray sat with his back to the trunk of a slender spruce, his knees bent and hands dangling between them. His attention remained focused on Scott and his woman. He shook his head as they kissed.

"I didn't have a choice." He glanced up and then away. "I'd gotten in with the wrong group of… friends, and they played hardball. It was either get them their money, or kiss my ass goodbye."

"So you decided, what? Pick one of us off and the other would fold?" Lucas said conversationally, while inside the volcano bubbled.

"No," Ray barked. "It wasn't like that. I thought I could just teach you a lesson. I didn't expect you to go and die on me." He dropped his legs, and then shifted them again, agitated.

"And what about the woman?" Lucas asked.

Ray's gaze flashed fearfully to Scott and his girl. "What woman?"

Lucas folded his arms and stared.

Ray looked up belligerently. "I don't know what you're talking about."

"Really?" Lucas crooked his brow. "'Cus I just read your mind. Are you sure you don't want to change your story? Restitution begins with the truth, my friend."

"Quit your preachin', it's too late to change what I've done."

Ray had made some serious mistakes, there was no denying that. Lucas had been shocked by what happened in his case, but horrified when he saw the replay of Ray deliberately hurting that dog, then killing the homeless man, and finally the ME working Lucas and Natalya's death. What happened to the kind and generous person they'd met all those years ago?

"I don't know what the future holds in store for you, but if you want any kind of chance at redeeming your soul, you need to make reparation."

He decided to let the other man stew it over for a while. "Stay put. I'm going to check on Scott. You better hope to hell he's going to be okay, or nothing's going to save your ass."

Turning away, Lucas stopped to grab the gun and remove temptation, then he started toward Scott but hesitated when he saw the kid shivering and staring into the forest.

"You okay?" He wasn't comfortable around kids in the first place, and with this one, it was even harder.

"Yeah," he said, his attention fixed into the distance.

Okay, that went well.

Lucas took a couple steps, swore under his breath, and turned back. *Practice what you preach, asshole.*

"I do know your dad," he blurted when Dustin looked at him. "You asked me that earlier and I never answered."

Dustin's eyes lit up and then turned angry. "Where is he? Why isn't he here? Doesn't he even care about us anymore?" His voice climbed, little chest heaving like a set of bellows. Tears formed on the ends of his lashes and dripped down his face.

Lucas felt like the slime on the bottom of a pond. "Of course he cares. More than anything."

He crouched down and met the boy's distraught gaze. "Your dad misses you so bad. If he knew you were here right now, nothing could keep him away."

He squeezed the child's arm and stood. "Running away won't solve your problems, kid. Your dad needs you to be a big boy and take care of your family now." He hesitated a moment, not sure what else he could say to help this family he'd wronged so badly. "Can you do that?"

Dustin looked down at his feet, then squared his shoulders and slowly nodded. "Yes, sir." He looked up with tear-bright eyes. "Can you tell my dad I love him?"

It was Lucas' turn to glance away. He swallowed the baseball in his throat and dipped his chin. "Yeah, kid. I'll do that."

They both stared into the forest for a moment, then Lucas clapped him lightly on the back, checked to make sure Ray was where he'd left him, and continued on to Scott.

"How you holding up?" He asked, and noticed the clasped hands of his friend and the woman doc.

Scott grinned, though it came off as more of a grimace as he shifted his leg to a more comfortable position. "Well, you know. A day in the park." He laughed, then held his side from the resulting pain.

Lucas didn't like the obvious signs of shock, but had to admit the woman had done a good job of patching him up. "Help should be here soon." He turned his gaze on the doc. "I'm going to have to disappear." He held out the gun, butt first. "Can you handle one of these?"

She looked at it like it was a snake, then reached out with trembling, bloodstained fingers and wrapped her hand around the handle. Lucas let go and she almost dropped it, but then she recovered and set it in her lap, her gaze fearful but determined. Hell of a woman.

He refocused on Scott, hating the fact there wasn't more he could do. "I won't be far. You need me, call. You got that?"

Scott looked as though there were things he wanted to say. He glanced at the others and nodded. "I miss you, bro."

Aw, shit.

Lucas coughed to cover his emotions, his chest one gigantic ache, and unfolded his wings.

"Me too," he muttered, then took flight, leaving his heart behind him.

Chapter 32

The beam from dozens of flashlights cut through the woods not long after, heralding the arrival of emergency services. Tracy pointed the police in Ray's direction and was more than happy to turn over the unwieldy gun, then stood by wringing her hands while the paramedics checked Scott over and prepared him for transport. She'd seen dozens of bodies in her years of work and never been as unsettled as she was now.

"How is he?" she asked when they had him loaded on a gurney and an intravenous started.

The female paramedic looked familiar and Tracy realized where she'd seen her; Jenny had brought her to their book club group one night.

"He's going to be fine. A little stiff and sore for a while, but nothing he can't handle." She smiled her reassurance, then turned back to the patient. "Hang on, we'll have you out of here soon."

Scott nodded, his gaze fuzzy now that the painkillers were kicking in. His head flopped sideways so that he could see her. "I'm sorry, baby. All my fault."

Tracy hurried forward, worried he was going to tip himself off the stretcher. She grasped his hand, careful of the tubes, and held it to her breast. "Don't. It's no more your fault than it is mine. Just let the medicine work. We'll talk later, okay?"

His head did a slow roll. "So many unnecessary deaths."

Hank, Lucas, Scott's sister, Natalya. The man being led away in cuffs had a lot to account for. Tears threatened, but she blinked them away. Crying could wait until later when she was alone.

The paramedic tucked a blanket around Scott's body. "We need to go."

Tracy nodded and leaned in to give Scott a lingering kiss. "I love you," she whispered.

His gaze softened. "Say it again."

Her chest tightened. She felt like she was having a panic attack, but then he squeezed her fingers and raised them to his lips and she was lost.

"I love you so very much," she said loudly and clearly, not giving a damn who heard her this time.

He raised his hand to the back of her head and pulled her close. "You and me, babe. It's going to be great." His mouth was warm and mobile and she closed her eyes the better to take in the exquisite touch.

The other paramedic cleared his throat. "We'd better leave. The police are waiting."

Tracy reluctantly lifted her head. "I'll be right behind you."

Scott's brows lowered, but there wasn't much choice. The trail was too narrow for anything more than single file. They moved out and Tracy went to follow, then thought of Dustin.

She glanced around and found him looking small and scared by the edge of the trail, a police officer close by. Scott's coat dangled off his shoulders and gave him a lost waif look with the sleeves dangling to his knees.

"You ready to go home? I bet your mom's going to be happy to see you." She smiled and held out her hand.

He gazed up at her, but didn't move, his eyes worried. "Am I going to be in trouble?"

Tracy's heart tugged for the poor kid. It wasn't fair. In one ill-fated moment he'd gone from being a child in a happy, healthy family to a young man tasked with picking up the pieces of their lives. It was a huge responsibility. And one Tracy planned to be a part of.

She leaned over and gave him a swift hug, grimacing at the bruising already occurring around his neck. "I don't really see that happening, but I promise to be there with you to help explain, okay?" They may have only just met, but the events of the last few hours had built a bond she hoped would last a lifetime.

Cold fingers wrapped around hers, the jacket bunched up his arm. "I'm ready."

A stream of light broke through the clouds and lit the path before them.

Mike and Lucas floated in silence above the scene playing out far below. Lucas felt a complex mix of gratitude and loss as Scott disappeared from view carried on a stretcher and followed by Ray in cuffs, a police officer on either side gripping his arms. He ached to be down there with his best friend. It was almost like losing a limb knowing they might never talk again. And Ray… the betrayal cut deep. They had trusted him and loved him like a father, and he'd repaid that with robbery and death. If not for Ray, he would still have a life.

He glanced at the hostile man by his side. They all would.

"Where were you?" he asked. "Your kid was in trouble and you were no where to be found." He half hoped Mike would take another shot at him. The tension was so thick between them already, something had to break.

Mike's gaze remained fixed on his son as he talked to the woman, then took her hand and followed the others down the trail. When everyone was gone and the forest was silent, he turned and faced Lucas.

"I went back to the Transition House. Do you want to know why?"

Lucas stiffened. There was something in the other man's expression that warned him he wasn't going to like where this conversation was heading.

"What did you do?" There was no reason for him to go back to the cabin. The only one there was... Natalya.

Lucas leaped forward, his hand wrapping around Mike's neck. "Where is she? What have you done, you son-of-a-bitch?"

Mike made no effort to protect himself. He just looked at Lucas over the grip around his throat and sneered, "You think you know pain and loss? Try losing a child."

Lucas loosened his hold and Mike reared backward, his wings ghostly in the night sky. "That's right, asshole. It wasn't enough that you took me away from my family. You also caused the death of my unborn child in that accident."

He veered away, his back rigid.

Lucas cursed Ray to hell. What a fricking mess. He rubbed the back of his neck. "Look, man, I'm sorry."

Mike's laugh was harsh as he swung around. "Not yet," he said, cryptically. "But you're going to be."

He took wing, spiraling upward. His final words, when they floated down, stopped Lucas' heart.

"An eye for an eye, my brother. You took what's mine. Now I have what's yours."

Afterword

Reviews are the lifeblood of any successful author. Without you, we can't be heard.

If you enjoy the story, please consider sharing on your favorite social media sites, as well as GoodReads and from wherever you've bought the book.

Thank you,
Jacquie Biggar
Jacqbiggar.com

About the Author

Jacquie Biggar is an author of the romantic suspense series, Wounded Hearts. This is Jacquie's first book in the paranormal genre.

Jacquie lives in paradise along the west coast of Canada with her family. She loves reading, writing, and flower gardening and swears she can't function without coffee, preferably at the beach with her sweetheart.

jacqbiggar.com
jbiggar@jacqbiggar.com

Also by Jacquie Biggar

Wounded Hearts Series

Tidal Falls

The Rebel's Redemption

Twilight's Encore

The Sheriff Meets His Match

Summer Lovin'